# The Ghost of Jeopardy Belle

Book Two

*Ghosts of Summerleigh* Series

By M.L. Bullock

## Dedication

To all the broken ones.

*The lady sleeps! Oh, may her sleep,*
*Which is enduring, so be deep!*
*Heaven have her in its sacred keep!*
*This chamber changed for one more holy,*
*This bed for one more melancholy,*
*I pray to God that she may lie*
*Forever with unopened eye,*
*While the pale sheeted ghosts go by!*

Excerpt from *The Sleeper*

Edgar Allan Poe, 1831

# *Prologue—Harper Belle*

## *Desire, Mississippi*
## *October 1942*

"Momma, Loxley is talking to her ghosts again," Addison announced sourly. The three of us girls were in the parlor reading the magazines that Mrs. Hendrickson gave me after her granddaughter left them behind when she returned to Mobile, but Addie was in a bad mood. Mostly because Loxley refused to move out of her current spot on the couch. Their bickering frustrated me. I wanted to finish this article about dreamy Frank Sinatra. I loved all his songs, especially Stardust, and I thought it might be a hoot to start a fan club right here in Desire. Other girls liked him too, but only I knew all his songs by heart. Whenever one of Sinatra's songs came on the radio, I sang it with all my might. I'd been saving up to buy a few of his records, maybe a whole album, but my record player would need a new needle soon. Aunt Dot gave me her RCA Victor because she bought herself a Wellington record player and radio for her birthday. It played three speeds and had a shiny wooden case. That was the last time I'd seen Aunt Dot, weeks ago. I missed her.

"Addison, stop," I warned her again in a whisper. My sister rubbed her nose with a hankie, but it didn't do much good. Her nose ran perpetually nowadays. Probably because it had rained for a whole week straight. Any kind of mold made her sick, and there were plenty of moldy spots in the old plantation we called home. Although I felt sympathy for her, I wished she would heed my warning. Instead, it appeared that her ill mood and Loxley's mischievousness would put us all in harm's way.

"No, I wasn't, Momma," Loxley called out innocently. "I was talking to Lenny, my pet."

"You girls keep quiet in there," Miss Augustine barked at us as she and Momma continued their gossiping and gin drinking and card playing at the kitchen table. I peeked around the corner from my spot on the floor. No, Momma wasn't moving, and she looked terrible today. Ever since Jeopardy's disappearance, something about her seemed wrong. Ann Marie Belle had always been a proud, pretty woman, beautiful like a model. Not anymore. She wore too much makeup, so much that it bordered on clownish, and she often had lipstick on her teeth. Her blond hair showed dark roots, and today she was still wearing her robe and pajamas. That was unheard of around here. Momma had always been the first one up in the morning and always dressed to the nines like a proper lady, especially on Sundays. But we didn't go to church anymore, and no one from First Baptist came to visit us. It was as if we were living on an island here at Summerleigh.

"Want to see my pet, Addison? I'll show you he's real." Loxley hopped off the loveseat but didn't budge from in front of it. With a perfectly innocent smile, she held out a pocket of her pinafore and offered Addison a peek inside.

Addie rubbed her nose again and waved her away. Her pale face crumpled miserably, and although she spent much of her time in bed, I thought perhaps she really needed to go for a lie-down. "Take your pet outside and give me my spot back, Loxley."

Loxley poked out her bottom lip and stomped her foot. "It's not your spot. I don't see your name on it. Isn't that right, Harper?" I didn't offer her any help. She was only making matters worse. I flipped the page of the magazine and tried to ignore them both. "Don't you want to see Lenny, Addison?"

Before Addison could reply, a green tree frog with big red eyes hopped out of Loxley's pocket and onto Addison's shoe. Addie screamed, and before I knew what was happening Momma stormed into the room with Miss Augustine in tow. Momma grabbed me first, picking me up by my hair, uncaring that I had nothing to do with the hoopla. Miss Augustine scolded her, "Now, Ann. Calm down. Remember what the doctor said about your nerves." But Momma didn't listen. She swung at my behind with her free hand, striking me not once but three times before she let me go. I yelped in surprise and pain while my sisters scrambled up the stairs.

"I told you to keep those girls quiet! Why don't you ever listen to me, Harper? You never listen!"

"I'm sorry, Momma. I'm sorry!" I yelled back, shocked at her violent attack. Miss Augustine stepped back and watched us from the doorway as if she too were afraid of Momma. Momma stomped toward me while I tried to back away. It was no use. There was no sense in fighting her, and I couldn't bring myself to raise a hand back. I closed my eyes and waited for the blow, thinking she'd slap me across the face. She liked doing that when I spoke an ill word to her. Or what she considered an ill word. A knock on the door put a stop to her intentions, and she squeezed my arm one good time before releasing me and tidying her robe. Without waiting to see who had arrived, I raced up the stairs to hide. The creaking floors moaned at my steps, but that did not slow me down. It was at that moment I decided Jeopardy's castle would become my castle, at least until she came home.

I ran up the attic stairs and closed the door behind me, tears streaming down my face. I didn't know where Addison was, but Loxley sat on Jeopardy's pallet crying for all she was worth. Her pretty face was streaked with dirty tears; her usually tidy braids were sagging in the heat of the attic.

"I'm sorry, Harper. I didn't know Lenny would jump out. He's never done that before. He's a good frog. Honest he is." I collapsed on the pallet and covered my face with my hands. My broken heart weighed heavy in my chest like a ton of lead. Even though she was the baby of the family, Loxley held me as I cried. After a few minutes of stroking my hair, she said, "I'm sorry, Harper. Really, I am. Did she hurt you real bad?" Her eyes were fearful and full of tears.

For her sake, I lied, "Not too bad." I sat up now and did what older sisters were supposed to do. I comforted Loxley, and we held one another a few minutes. "Loxley, tell me the truth. Do you ever see Jeopardy? I have to know. Is Jeopardy here...is she a ghost?"

Loxley slowly shook her head. "I never see Jeopardy, but I look for her, Harper. Honest, I have tried. Daddy comes sometimes, but he doesn't talk to me. I can see his mouth moving, but I can't hear him. He looks sad now. And he doesn't smile anymore."

"Is he...does he look like he always did?" *He's not bloody, is he? Tell me he doesn't look like a bloody fiend.*

"Yes, he looks the same." She wrinkled her neat blond brows and said, "But he's not the only one here."

"The lady ghost? Do you see her?"

"Not much, but the other night I heard tapping on my window." She tapped at the air. "It was real soft, like how Jeopardy used to tap on your window when she wanted to come inside. But when I got up to look for Jeopardy, it was just the boy, the mean one who comes around sometimes. He used to stay upstairs, but now he goes all over the place, even outside. He has black eyes, Harper, and he scares me. He scratches me sometimes."

I didn't have any sisterly advice, so I just nodded thoughtfully, and suddenly her eyes brimmed with tears again. "He...he made me cut up your dress, Harper. I'm so sorry. He said I had to do it or something horrible would happen to you. He gave me the scissors."

Stunned at her confession, I held her and said nothing else. All this time, I had believed that Jeopardy had destroyed the dress Momma had let me borrow for the Harvest Dance. I believed that Jeopardy wanted to hurt me, and she'd been innocent the whole time. Loxley and I both gasped as the attic door creaked open, but it was only Addison who stepped inside. I waved at her to join us on the pallet.

She didn't say, "I'm sorry." Addison rarely apologized, but just her being here was proof of her repentance. I held her too, and the three of us sobbed together until we were all cried out. I opened the window to cool the room, and soon my sisters and I fell asleep. No one came to look for us. Not like the day Aunt Dot came to tell us that Daddy had died. I shuddered to think of him bleeding out pinned inside his old truck. Momma didn't like coming up here, not since that ghost pushed her down the stairs. And I knew it was a ghost because I'd seen her with my own two eyes. The door hung open for a while and didn't move again. But just as I closed my eyes, I saw the door open wider.

"Jeopardy?" I asked as sleep took me under. It was then that I saw him. I hovered between sleep and wakefulness, and I was unable to move or speak. I couldn't cry out or warn my sisters. It was as if I were paralyzed. At first, I saw a black form—blacker than a crow's wing, blacker than the darkness that enveloped the attic. But then the blackness became something else. It was a gray mist and had a shape, a boy's shape. And now, by some strange magic, I could see him clear as day.

He stared at me with perfect hatred, and then a black smile crossed his face.

# *Chapter One—Jerica Poole*

## *Present Day*

Sawdust floated in the sunlight that shone through the new parlor windows. The roof repairs were finally finished, but I was a long way from completing Summerleigh's restoration. The combined scents of fresh paint and new wood thrilled my soul, and I pretended that the progress made the Belle home feel lighter. Happier. But I knew I was only fooling myself. Despite the activity, the constant stream of people coming in and out of the old plantation, I couldn't shake the feeling that we weren't alone here...and we weren't wanted. I couldn't understand it. Jeopardy and John Jeffrey Belle were together now. Together and free from the sins of the past. Why would they linger at Summerleigh?

And now Ben Hartley was standing in the Great Room, and he wasn't happy. "Please, Jerica. Please reconsider what you're doing. You have done enough here. Harper never expected you to do all this. She wanted you to bring Jeopardy home, and you did that. Take what's left of the money—she wanted you to have it—take it and go home."

I couldn't believe what I was hearing. I wiped the sweat from my brow and tugged off my gloves, shoving them in my back pocket. "I don't understand, Ben. I thought you would want this. You love Summerleigh...I know you do."

"I loved Harper, Jerica. Not this place. I never loved this place," he confessed as he cast his eyes around the room and then at the ceiling. Yes, I heard the footsteps too, but it was only Jesse checking out the floors on the second level.

"Is it the money, Ben? I'm staying on budget, and there's plenty left to complete the repairs."

"It's not that. You can do what you want with the money, as that was Harper's wish. But what happens after you finish all this? Do you plan to stay here at Summerleigh? Raise a family? What are your intentions?"

Before I could respond, Jesse walked through the front door with his new helper, Emanuel, trailing behind him. If Jesse wasn't upstairs walking around, who was? I gulped as Ben stared back at me, obviously hoping for an answer.

*Get a grip, Jerica Poole. There are people all over the place in here today.*

"I'll be honest, Ben. I don't have an end game, but I need to do this." I waved my hands at the construction happening around us. "I want to honor Harper's generosity, leave a legacy in her name. And I don't want the Belle girls to be forgotten, not Harper and not Jeopardy. None of them. They deserve better than that."

Ben shook his head sadly and sighed. He clutched his old-fashioned hat in his hand and flinched at the sound of the nail gun going off in the other room.

"Come in the kitchen. You have to see what we've accomplished." I hoped showing him our progress would appease him or at least make him happier. I hated seeing him upset. Ben had been Harper's friend, and I cared about him. I didn't quite understand their relationship and was certainly curious about it, but I wasn't one to pry. "The original Wedgewood stove couldn't be saved, but Jesse helped me find this replacement. It's modern but looks close to the original; it's gas, but the connectors won't corrode. I didn't want a bunch of chrome in here, so I went with the original white enamel for the stove and refrigerator. Pretty neat, huh?"

I lived in Ben's old home now, the former caretaker's cottage, and I knew he loved vintage kitchens. When I moved into the cottage, I'd been amazed at the neat metal cabinets and mid-century modern table and chairs.

"Yes, it's all very nice. I should go now. Thank you for your time. If you don't mind, I'd like to go for a walk in the garden and maybe visit Jeopardy's new memorial stone before I head back to the hotel. I'm leaving for Jackson in the morning."

I didn't want to cause him more hurt, but I didn't understand his sadness. "Of course, Ben. You're always welcome here."

He opened the door and paused. "Goodbye, Jerica," he said. "I wish you the best of luck."

*Why did that sound so foreboding?*

"Bye, Ben." Then I had an idea. "Why don't you stop by the cottage before you leave? It's almost four o'clock, and we'll all be knocking off for the weekend in a few minutes. I've got to pay everyone, but maybe we could talk after?"

Without looking back, he said, "We'll see," and then he closed the door behind him and left me standing in the newly renovated kitchen by myself. That sounded exactly like something my father would have said—and it always meant no.

"Okay," I called to him through the closed door. I was mystified by the entire exchange.

"Am I interrupting anything?" Jesse's deep voice surprised me, and I smiled as I spun around to face him. Jesse Clarke was a handsome man, that was for sure. In the three months I'd been here, we'd become close. We were nothing more than good friends, although there was always the temptation for more, at least on my part. Of course, twenty-six-year-old Jerica was much more careful than the Jerica who had gotten married right out of high school.

Jesse had proven to be a skilled carpenter, and I was glad to have his help with Summerleigh. I'd yet to see his boat—or more precisely, the hull of his boat, as he described it—but he'd asked me to join him for a bite to eat tonight. He wanted to try out some new steakhouse on Highway 98. I tried not to think of the dinner as a date; we'd eaten lunch together a few times, but we'd always talked about some project related to the house, so I'd never considered those dates.

"No. Just talking to myself. Ben just left, and he didn't seem happy with my decision to stay at Summerleigh."

"He told you not to stay?"

"He thinks I should leave. I get the feeling that he thinks I'm doomed if I stay," I replied with another nervous laugh. "Am I missing something?"

Jesse leaned over the shiny new farmhouse sink and stared out the window. "I'll talk to him. Which way did he go?"

"He said he was going to visit Jeopardy's memorial, take a walk in the garden. He's acting pretty strange."

"Huh, he must have been moving pretty fast because I don't see him now. Well, that's Ben for you, Jerica. Don't take any of what he says to heart. He's probably like a lot of people; he thinks the place is...unlucky."

"You started to say cursed, didn't you?" I shuffled my feet and shoved my hands in my blue jean pockets. "Is Summerleigh cursed?" Again I felt the sensation that someone was standing behind me, but I didn't turn around.

"No. I don't believe in curses, and neither should you."

"I know you believe in ghosts. We didn't dream that up."

"No, we didn't. Ree-Ree is my cousin, remember? So of course I believe in the supernatural. But like I said, I wouldn't put much stock in anything Ben said. He's an unhappy old man. Summerleigh is just a place, a dot on a map. Like any old house, it has seen its share of tragedy. What you're doing here is a good thing, Jerica. I'm happy to be a part of it. It's been a dream come true for me. I've always loved this place, and working in here, seeing it come back to life...I can't tell you how lucky I feel to be a part of it."

I smiled at hearing his words, but his confession also worried me. What if Jesse's affection for me wasn't really for me? What if it was because he loved this house so much? *God, what are you doing, Jerica? Stop overthinking it.* He was right. I was letting Ben's moodiness affect me, and I really shouldn't. Things had been going so well. I got word that my ex-husband was right where he needed to be, in jail, and my friend Anita was planning to drive down and visit me for Christmas.

"What do you know about Ben and Harper? I mean, what's their connection? I get the feeling that for Ben, she was the one that got away. Am I right?"

He smiled slyly. "I'll tell you all about it tonight. Pick you up at seven?"

"Sure, you can pick me up, but wouldn't you rather I just meet you there? I would hate for you to come all this way when you live so close to the restaurant," I said as I locked the back door.

"I'm not sure how the dating scene is in Virginia, Jerica Poole, but here in Mississippi it is customary for a gentleman to pick up a lady," he replied with a playful wink.

"Oh, it's a date-date," I said softly as my stomach flip-flopped from either nerves or excitement.

Jesse leaned back against the sink and crossed his arms. That was his move when he was unsure about something like my choice of stain or my idea for the new spindles on the staircase. "If you think it's better that we don't call it a date, I'll understand. Or if you want to cancel, I'll understand that too."

By the tone of his voice, I knew neither was true at all. And I didn't want to cancel. "I'm not canceling anything, Jesse Clarke. I'll be ready at seven o'clock, but I'd better go pay the guys. Will you make sure nobody is left upstairs? I thought I heard someone stomping around up there earlier."

"Sure, I'll do a walk-through, pack up the equipment and lock up the place."

"Great," I said with an awkward smile. "I'll see you later."

I tried not to skip out of the kitchen like a silly teenager.

## *Chapter Two—Jerica*

Ben never arrived at the cottage; I hadn't really expected him to, but I worried about him nonetheless. I didn't see any extra cars in my driveway, but Summerleigh was a big place. At least there were a lot of woods around here to hide a vehicle. I walked to Jeopardy's monument between Summerleigh and the cottage but didn't see Ben anywhere. Not on the bench under the oak tree and not strolling the graveled walkways. I'd replaced the previous obscure marker with something more appropriate. The new monument read, "Jeopardy Belle, Beloved Daughter of John Jeffrey Belle. Together Always." Rumor had it that Ann Belle had placed the former stone there in memory of her lost daughter, but I couldn't be sure. I believed the ghost of Jeopardy Belle visited here from time to time, though her body now rested next to her sisters. Once in a while, I thought I heard her young, raspy voice, a voice I would know almost as well as my own or Marisol's. But I never saw her.

After walking to the potting shed and down the path a bit, I decided that Ben had most certainly left, and I hurried back to my cottage to get ready for my first official date with Jesse Clarke.

Me? Dating again? I couldn't believe it. While my hair dried, I ransacked my closet for something appropriate. Should I stick with blue jeans or wear a dress? I settled on the latter. I'd bought a few dresses from a boutique in Lucedale, and now I had the chance to take one off the hanger. The dress was made of a soft material, mossy green with a scoop neck and cap sleeves. I had strong arms, and after all the work we'd been doing, I was proud of how toned they looked.

The phone downstairs rang, which was so rare that I had to think about what it was I was hearing. I hurried downstairs to answer it. "Hello?"

"Hello, Jerica? This is Hannah Ray. Do you remember me?" Of course I remembered Renee's friend, the psychic who helped us connect with Ann and John Jeffrey Belle. During the process of helping find justice for Jeopardy Belle, I discovered that my daughter was close by. In fact, it was Hannah who let me know that Marisol lingered near me often and listened to me whenever I spoke to her. After setting things right for Harper, contacting Marisol was all I could think about. Talking to my baby again seemed like a dream come true, but the past few months I had dragged my heels about contacting Hannah. Renee had brought her up to me once or twice, but I hesitated. I guessed a part of me was afraid that if I did communicate with Marisol, she would leave me forever. Didn't I want her to be at peace and happy? Yes, but I had to admit that I was selfish enough to want to keep Marisol close to me. Yes, I could admit that, even if only to myself.

"Of course, Hannah. Glad to hear from you. I've been meaning to call you, but..."

"Jerica, I have to warn you," she blurted out. "There's a shifting occurring at Summerleigh. I can feel it, and I'm hearing disturbing things, to put it bluntly. Very disturbing. Have you been experiencing any activity there?"

"I haven't seen any ghosts, if that's what you're asking. I think Jeopardy and John Jeffrey Belle are at peace now, Hannah. You said it yourself. I haven't seen any sign of them."

"It's not about the Belles..." Her voice crackled on the phone.

"What? I can't hear you, Hannah. Are you on your cell phone?"

"It's really important that you listen to me, Jer... I don't know what's causing this disturbance, the renovations or something else, but things are stirred up. Spiritual things. I am concerned that—"

And then the phone went dead.

I stared at the receiver of the old-fashioned Princess phone and clicked the button up and down, but there was no sound. Not even a dial tone. I hung the phone up and picked it up again, but still nothing. The knock at the door pulled me away from the strangeness of the moment. It was Jesse. I recognized his knock. He always knocked three times, and it was always a firm, confident knock. Strange that I would know that.

Opening the door with a forced smile, I said, "Hey, Jesse. Come in. I was just on the phone with Hannah, but the line died. Give me just a second." I picked up the phone again and this time got a dial tone. Whatever happened, the phone company had apparently corrected it quickly. I flipped through the little phone book next to the phone, searching for Hannah's number, and dialed her back. She quickly answered.

"Jerica, thank goodness. I was just about to drive over there. I thought...never mind. Do me a favor, stay out of Summerleigh tonight. Don't go in until I get there."

I turned my back to Jesse to hide my growing apprehension. "I'm not going to be here, Hannah. I have a date with Jesse. Is there something I should know about? What's going on? Tell me plainly, please."

"I will, but I have the feeling that I need to talk to you face-to-face. Are you gonna be home later tonight, or should I come in the morning?"

"Morning works for me. How about around nine o'clock? Come to my place, the caretaker's cottage."

"Sounds great, but remember what I told you. Please, stay out of the house tonight."

"Okay." She hung up the phone, and I put the receiver down.

"What's up?"

I turned to face him and forced another smile, despite the fact that the hair on my arms stood up a mile high. It was then that I noticed he was carrying a bouquet of wildflowers, which were my absolute favorite. "Hey, are those for me?"

He gave me a curious look. I knew he wanted to know about my phone call, but I wasn't going to go there. I'd already set our date off on the wrong foot by running back to the phone to call Hannah. Why make it worse?

"Nope. I found them outside."

"Are you for real?"

"Of course not. I bought them for you. Unless you don't want them. I guess I could give them to someone else."

"You wouldn't dare," I said as I grinned back at him. And then I asked playfully, "How is it that you, master carpenter and five-star hash slinger, are still single? Is it because you like to play guitar on your first date?"

"I see my cousin has been bragging about my musical skills. I'm not the best guitar player in George County, but I enjoy playing even if I do hit a wrong note every now and then."

I laughed, happy to think about something besides that phone call. "I'm sure Renee's exaggerating. I bet you are a stellar performer." I accepted the flowers and went to put them in the sink, but Jesse caught my hand and gently pulled me back.

"I might be rushing this, but I've been thinking about it all day. Hell, I've been thinking about it for months. I'd like to kiss you, Jerica." He was so close to me I could smell his skin. It smelled clean and had a touch of cedar to it. His hand was warm in mine, and he looked a sight in his gray dress pants and charcoal gray dress shirt.

Clutching the flowers, I looked up at him. "What have you been thinking about?" I asked as I stepped a little closer to him. There were only a few inches between us now.

In a husky voice, he pulled me closer and whispered, "This." And then his soft lips were on mine. It wasn't quite a chaste kiss, but he didn't push himself on me. It was sweet and warm and a kiss that I would probably be thinking about long after this night was over.

Without moving away, I bowed my head a little. I just couldn't meet his eyes yet. I didn't want him to see how much I enjoyed it. "I have to admit I've thought about it too."

He asked even more softly, "Should we do it again?"

"If we do it again, I'm not sure we will actually make it to dinner. And I think... I think..." And then I caught a glimmer of light out of the corner of my eye. "What is that?" I pulled away from Jesse and walked to the window. The light flashed through the window again, but it wasn't coming from my house or the yard.

The light was low and steady now. And it was coming from the attic of Summerleigh.

## *Chapter Three—Jerica*

"You did the walk-through, right? There weren't any lights on when you left, were there?" I asked Jesse, keeping my eyes on the light that was pulsating in the attic. The colors changed subtly, first white, then blue, and then the light took on a strange purple hue and turned white again. It was almost as if some disco ball spun around up there.

*A weird, otherworldly disco ball.*

"Yeah, like I always do." He was beside me now, both of us staring at the attic window. "I'd better go check that out. It's possible that I missed one, but I don't know what the hell could make that kind of light. Maybe one of the guys is having a joke on us, but I'm pretty sure I would've seen any light when I pulled up. Might be that we have an intruder."

*Or it might be something else. No way was that a burglar.* Then I remembered Hannah's admonition. *Stay out of the house tonight.* Jesse walked to the front door as if he had every intention of going up there this very minute to see who might be plundering around in the attic.

"Wait. When Hannah called, she warned me that there was a strange energy at Summerleigh tonight. She warned me not to go inside. She's coming over tomorrow to talk to me about what she knows."

"What? What do you mean she warned you?"

"That was her on the phone when you came in. She wanted me to stay out of the house until she could go with me. There's something happening, Jesse. She was pretty adamant that I stay out of there." I chewed my bottom lip and twisted a strand of hair around my finger as I talked.

"I would never call Hannah a thief or a criminal, but it seems awful convenient that she would ask you to stay out of the house and now we see a strange light in the attic. If you don't want to go inside, that's okay, but I should go check it out. I mean, I am the general contractor on this job."

Was he pulling rank on me? I was never going to go for that. "If you go, I go." I grabbed my keys and turned off the lights. "It's probably just some..." No. I had no explanation for it. "I don't know." I really didn't know, but I was about to break my promise to Hannah. I locked the caretaker's cottage, and we walked past Jesse's truck down the gravel path to the back door of Summerleigh. Walking into the house through this door always felt like an intrusion, but the front porch still needed some work in a few places. So for safety's sake, this was the best option.

Before Jesse could take out his key, I put mine in the lock and turned it. The new lock was silent as the grave, and the new door didn't squeak or make a sound. Without turning on any lights, we eased the door shut and hurried through the kitchen and into the parlor. I held Jesse's hand as we waited to hear evidence of an intruder. We didn't have long to wait. Footsteps raced up the second-floor stairs, and I could hear someone running down the hall.

Those weren't the footsteps of a man or woman. Those were the footsteps of a child. We paused at the bottom of the stairs.

"Why don't you stay down here?" Jesse suggested. "Just in case."

"In case what? If there's really someone here, I want to know about it."

"Let's move quietly, then. Take off your shoes."

I kicked off my high heels and quietly set them out of the way. Together, Jesse and I climbed the stairs, pausing after every squeak the old floors made. We'd replaced some of the wood, but most of the staircase was actually in good shape. We stopped at the landing and waited again. We heard nothing now. Whoever was up there had to know we were coming because they didn't make a sound. *And we have no weapons!* Still holding hands, we stood on the top-floor landing. The long hallway stretched in front of us, but sure enough, there was a low light shining from beneath the attic door. There was movement in the light, as if someone were silently walking back and forth. I clutched Jesse's hand tighter, and he glanced at me reassuringly with a finger to his lips.

This was wrong. It felt wrong. There was such a heaviness in Summerleigh now; it felt much heavier than earlier. The place had felt off for days, as if someone were watching every move I made. But now it was like the entire focus of the house was on Jesse and me, and that focus was deadly.

With faux bravado, I blurted out, "Who's there?" To my shock, the movement stopped and the light faded. Jesse released my hand and eased down the hall, leaving me behind. His dress shoes were quiet, but the grit on the floor made a light crunching sound beneath them.

*Ugh. I wish I could wash my feet before I put my shoes back on.* The doors to all the rooms were open, and blackness poured out from all of them. But I wasn't fooled by the apparent emptiness. We were not alone. I could feel the presence of someone else here. Someone who wanted to remain hidden. Someone who didn't believe we belonged here. I didn't dare call out again since the element of surprise was no longer on our side. We hurried to the door and I reached for it, but Jesse shook his head. He leaned his ear against the wood and listened.

Nothing. We heard nothing at all.

I put my hand on the old-fashioned doorknob and turned it with the slowest of movements, but the door wouldn't budge. Because my eyes had adjusted to the darkness, I could see Jesse's face clearly. He shot me a curious look, so I removed my hand and he gave it a try. No luck. It was as if it were locked from the inside. And there was no key to it. Who had locked the door? He turned the chipped enamel knob again, rattling it furiously now. The sound echoed through the empty hallway.

"We know you're in there. Open this door," Jesse said authoritatively as he knocked on it.

Nobody answered. But then I heard the sound of a long, heavy breath in my ear. And with the breath came the moving of air. Every door on the top hallway began to slam shut. Not together, as you might expect if a blast of wind blew through the house. No. They closed hard, slamming shut one at a time until there were no doors left open. And suddenly the attic door swung wide open and Jesse nearly fell into it. I ran after him and we stood in the attic room, our hearts pounding as we looked around wildly, but there was no one and nothing to see. Nothing except some trunks, a half-dozen stacked crates, an old wooden rocking horse with an angry face, a rusty birdcage and a turn-of-the-century mannequin. There was more junk in here than I remembered from the last time I'd been up here, and certainly more than when Jeopardy Belle claimed this place and dubbed it her castle room.

"Hello? Who's in here? We saw your light. Don't hide from us." Still not a word, but then my left hand felt cold as if some unseen person had grabbed it. I caught my breath and lifted my hand to look at it. Now my entire arm was cold—no, it was freezing. "Jesse. Something's touching me. I can feel it."

With a worried expression, he said, "I better get you out of here. Come on, let's go. I've got a flashlight in the truck. I can come back and..." His words trailed off as he stared down the hallway.

My eyes followed his, but at first I didn't see what he was looking at. Then the strange light reappeared, illuminating the little figure. Yes, I could see him now. The little boy from my dream, the one Harper saw.

The light vanished, and only the boy remained. He wore knee britches and a fitted jacket with black socks and boots. His hair was black and combed carefully to the side. His face was pale, but his eyes...oh, his eyes were horrible and as black as two endless wells. And then he opened his mouth as if to scream, only no sound came out. His mouth was so wide, and it was black too. There was no doubt that what we were seeing was not a human child. This creature was a ghost, a phantom.

As I stared unblinkingly, I noticed that he did not move a muscle but stared back, his head bent down a little further now.

His dark eyes focused on me. He wanted me to die. He wanted Horrible Things to happen to me. I clutched Jesse's hand again and felt him grabbing at mine. As long as we were together, if we stayed together, we would be okay. I wanted to believe that, but the thing was not moving. His head bent even lower and he squatted on his haunches as if he would pounce on us like a wild animal. Suddenly all of the doors began slamming, opening and shutting furiously. The movement was so violent I feared they would fall off the hinges. What if he tore the place apart and brought Summerleigh down upon our heads?

From somewhere deep within me, a scream erupted. "No! Stop it!" And suddenly, he vanished.

The attic door swung silently closed and we were alone again, but the air crackled still. My cry had stopped him, but I did not believe he would be gone forever. We had to go, and we had to go now. Hannah Ray had been right. We should never have come here.

Jerking Jesse's hand, I yelled at him, "Come on!"

Together we raced down the hall. I prayed that the boy would stay away and not pop out at us or try to stop us. Before running downstairs, I paused to look behind me, and that's when I saw the other one.

The ghost of a young woman, a teenager, wore a long white dress with a faded rose at her bosom. The front of her gown was marred with dark stains, and her dark hair fell over her pale shoulders as she hovered near the attic. *Oh God! She had no feet. She has no feet!* She reached out to us and began to move slowly toward us.

"Run!" I screamed at Jesse as we hurried out of Summerleigh. I forgot my shoes and didn't remember to breathe until we got into his truck. I was pretty sure the gravel had cut my feet, but I didn't stop to look at the wounds. We sat panting in the vehicle, but this wasn't far enough. We had to go farther; we had to get out of there. I glanced up at the attic, which was dark now, and imagined I could feel the boy's dead black eyes watching us.

"Get me out of here, Jesse."

"Where to?" he asked as he cranked the truck and made the trip around the circular drive.

"I don't care. Anywhere."

We didn't talk again until we made it to Lucedale.

## *Chapter Four—Harper*

Momma spent most of her days sleeping because she spent most of her nights drinking. Even Miss Augustine hadn't been to the house in weeks. Knowing Momma, they'd gotten into a big row over some silly thing like who would become the next Miss Magnolia or what the preacher's new wife would wear to the fellowship Sunday next. Not that we would attend. We hadn't been to church in so long.

Loxley spent all her time creating "art" on the floor of her room and the porch and anywhere she found a blank canvas. I'd been happy for her when Mrs. Loper surprised her with a box of chalk for her birthday, but it quickly became a source of contention around the house. Momma didn't like it when she drew on the floor. I didn't either, but I didn't think it merited a spanking. Not Momma's idea of a spanking, anyway.

We were stretched for school clothes this year. Addison and I had both had a growth spurt, and our skirts were shorter than they should have been, which would no doubt land us in the principal's office if I didn't fix them soon. Mr. Alfred was a notorious stickler for proper skirt lengths. In fact, it was said that he kept a measuring tape in his desk at all times. Only Loxley appeared locked in time and hadn't grown an inch, except her hair. One night, I spent my time letting out the hems of our skirts and giving my sisters haircuts. Loxley cried at the idea of cutting her hair, but I bribed her with a peppermint stick, one I'd kept since Christmas, and I had to promise to cut no more than an inch. Before tucking her into bed, I braided her hair, and she drifted off to sleep soon after. Her sweet face was all sticky when I kissed her cheek.

Every night when we got home from school, I hoped I would see Aunt Dot pull into the driveway and come to our rescue. But there was no sign of my aunt, and since the phone had been disconnected, I had no way of calling her to let her know how dire our situation was. Just last night the power went out, and I had a sneaking suspicion that this was further proof Momma was not paying the bills and was spending what little money we did have on gin and cigarettes. I'd scrounged up some candles in a bureau drawer, but that wouldn't last long. I didn't look forward to taking cold showers either.

After I finished fixing our skirts, I was just about ready to go to bed when I heard someone tapping on the front door. It was almost nine o'clock, and we didn't have callers this late unless it was something serious. I pulled my robe around myself to cover up my flimsy nightgown. I even took the trouble to button the top four buttons. Luckily, I hadn't set my hair yet. The visitor tapped again. *Maybe it's Aunt Dot? Or Jeopardy?*

"I'm coming." I was suddenly happy at the possibility of seeing someone I loved. I hurried down the hallway before stepping into the Great Room. I saw no sign of Momma, which meant she hadn't heard the door. The house was so dark without any electricity, and I regretted not bringing a candle with me. With my hand on the door, I felt a sudden sense of dread and said, "Who is it?"

"Mr. Daughdrill. Open the door, Harper."

I almost never saw my grandfather, and for him to visit our home without Momma preparing us first was highly unusual. I opened the door but kept the screen door latched and said, "Yes, sir?"

"Where's your Momma? She's not answering my phone calls; the operator says the phone has been disconnected. Is that true?" My grandfather was a tall man, probably the tallest man I'd ever seen. He wore a loose gray suit and no hat. Mr. Daughdrill had salt-and-pepper hair, which he kept short, and he was always neat. Even his fingernails were neat. You'd never see dirty nails on him, not like Daddy, who always liked working with his hands. I wondered what Mr. Daughdrill did for a living, but I never had the courage to ask him.

Almost happy to relay the negative report, I answered him, "Yes, sir. The phone is out, and we don't have any electricity. I'm sure it's an oversight on Momma's part. She's been so upset, what with Jeopardy being gone and all."

"Open the door, Harper."

As I flipped the hook up, I noticed I didn't have to stand on tiptoe anymore to open the latch. I stepped out of the way as Mr. Daughdrill walked inside Summerleigh. For the briefest second, I thought I heard footsteps overhead. But it was probably just my imagination, the old house settling in the autumn heat or some such thing.

"Where is your Momma now?" He pulled off his suit coat and hung it on the bare coat rack.

"I think she's in her bedroom. Do you want me to get her?"

"No. That's not necessary. My, you've become a beautiful young woman, Harper Louise. So much like your Momma." His cool hand touched my face ever so briefly. "You go to bed now," he said, smiling at me in the half-light.

I shivered but smiled back politely. I rarely received compliments, and to be compared with Momma was certainly a compliment.

"All right, Mr. Daughdrill. Good night."

"Harper?"

"Yes, sir?" I paused in the doorway of the Great Room that led to our bedrooms. He was only a few feet behind me now.

"I wouldn't mind if you called me Grandfather. I wouldn't mind it at all."

I smiled again and answered, "Yes, sir. Grandfather. Good night."

I hurried off to my room and closed the door behind me. My heart was pounding in my chest, and I heard my grandfather's footsteps travel down the hall to

Momma's room. He didn't yell at her, but his voice was loud and stern at first. I couldn't quite make out the words. Momma cried and argued with him, but the house soon grew quiet and I fell asleep.

I woke before dawn, surprised to find that Momma was up too. She wore one of her favorite dresses today, the blue and white checkered one that she usually wore only when Daddy was coming home. It broke my heart to see it. Despite her attempt to put on a happy face, she still wasn't quite together, but at least she was not wearing a robe and didn't have lipstick on her teeth. Her hair still needed to be fixed, but she wore a smattering of makeup and had taken the time to put on pantyhose and her newest heels. She had a ladder in her hose, but I wasn't going to be the one to tell her that.

As I walked into the kitchen, she smiled sweetly at me and said, "Good morning, Harper Louise. I made y'all some scrambled eggs this morning. Would you like some toast with your eggs?"

I stared at her, not believing what I was hearing and seeing. Momma never made us breakfast. She rarely cooked dinner, and for her to be up and ready to take us to school was just too much of a coincidence. I attributed her change of behavior to my grandfather's visit last night.

"Yes, ma'am. I'll go see if Addison and Loxley are ready yet."

"You do that. I'll get that toast going." I stared at her as she sliced hunks of bread from the stale loaf and placed them on a baking sheet. We didn't have a toaster, so we had to make toast the old-fashioned way in our house. She smiled up at me and said, "Don't dawdle, Harper. Get going. I don't want you girls to be late. And don't forget to put on pantyhose. You're too old to go around with bare legs."

"Yes, Momma." I hated wearing pantyhose. In fact, not many girls wore hose anymore except for formal occasions. Bobby socks were all the fashion, but I didn't have any of them or any saddle shoes. Maybe one day, if I was smart enough to find a job, I would have my own money and could buy the clothes that I dreamed of, like the ones in the magazines. What girl wouldn't want the latest styles? One day, I would own a whole collection of floral scarves to wear around my neck and hair.

Addison felt ill, but she usually did before any kind of social activity. It was her nerves, I reminded her, and I coached her through her many worries. Loxley dressed quickly and hurried off to the kitchen to enjoy her breakfast. Addison had another spell of retching, but I helped her clean up. When I walked into the kitchen with her, I was surprised to see my grandfather sitting at the table as if he intended to take breakfast along with us Belle girls. I didn't like that he was sitting in Daddy's chair, but nobody else seemed to mind so I kept silent.

*Momma should say something! She should ask him to move!* I glanced at my mother's face and could hardly believe the transformation in her. But no matter how hard she tried, I would never trust her again. The memory of my mother striking me and picking me up by my hair was still fresh in my mind, even though it had happened weeks ago. I wondered what my grandfather would think about her behavior.

"Good morning, girls," he said politely to us as he opened his newspaper and placed it beside his plate.

In unison we replied, "Good morning." He smiled at us all but winked at me. Momma saw it but didn't say a word. She kept her eyes on her plate and didn't eat anything at all.

"Eat your food, ladies. You need a good breakfast to do well in school. I hear you'll be graduating in a few years, Harper Louise. Tell me, what are your plans for when you graduate? Are you going off to college?"

I scooped up a forkful of eggs and said nervously, "I would like to, but I don't know if we can afford that, Grandfather." I popped the eggs in my mouth as my Momma's eyes widened. She drew in a sharp breath and sat up straight in her chair staring at her father and me. Addison and Loxley eyeballed me but kept eating. None of us girls were allowed to call him Grandfather, none except Jeopardy, but now I had that privilege. I instantly regretted using the term.

"You leave that to me, dear girl. If you want to go to college, I'll make sure that you do." He reached for my hand and squeezed it. His hand felt clammy and cold, and I wasn't used to being touched. There weren't many hugs administered in this house, not since Daddy died. Once upon a time, Jeopardy had been one to hug you, to show affection in sudden and wonderful ways, but before she disappeared, those spontaneous hugs had become as rare as Momma's.

"Girls, let's go now. It's time we were off to school." Momma still hadn't eaten a bite but sipped her coffee quickly and stood, straightening her dress.

"Oh no, dear. You can't go out looking like that. Just look at your hair, Ann." He clucked his tongue as Momma's hands flew to her unbrushed locks.

"I'll wear a scarf, Father."

"I don't think a scarf will help. I'll take these girls to school and come back when I'm done. I think it would be good for us to have a chat about Harper's future. Don't you?"

I saw Momma's hands clench by her sides in tight fists, and she wobbled in her shoes. Would she faint? Her face reddened, and she did something I had never seen before—she defied Mr. Daughdrill. "I'll take my girls to school, Father, and I'll be right back. Hurry up, girls. Let's go."

Loxley whined about not finishing her breakfast, but she grabbed her toast and followed behind Momma. I cast an eye behind me to my grandfather's face. He was clearly furious, but it was the silent kind of fury, the kind I'd seen on Momma's face so frequently. And then he called out to us, "I will be picking you girls up. Look for my car after school." Momma didn't argue back but took me by the hand and led us out of the house and to her car.

I expected her to say something to us, something about the weirdness of our grandfather being at our kitchen table this morning. Perhaps an apology or some declaration of how things would change and how she would try harder to be a better mother to us all, but she said nothing. She clutched the steering wheel so hard her hands were white, and I noticed she wore no gloves. *Momma always wears gloves when she drives the car.* She pulled up in front of the school, and even though we were thirty minutes early, we got out of the car and watched her pull away. Momma looked at me with an expression I could not interpret and then left us behind. She was gone by the time I thought to ask her for lunch money, but luckily for my sisters, I had fifty cents in my purse.

We waited on the bench outside the front door of the school until the principal arrived and unlocked the door. He was polite and made a sweet comment about us being anxious for classes to start. Other teachers arrived a few minutes later, but none of the adults said a word to us about Jeopardy. I could tell they were curious—or perhaps they felt sorry for us. I wasn't sure.

The day did not go as planned. My hose kept falling down, and I had to retreat into the ladies' restroom to pull them back up more than once. I finally gave up about halfway through the day and went into a bathroom stall and removed them completely, shoving them in my purse. My bare legs felt cool, and the strange defiance of going without hose thrilled me slightly. I would never be as defiant as Jeopardy, but I was learning in my own way how to show the same kind of bravery she did.

*How I miss you, Jeopardy Belle!*

Thinking about being at school without her was too much. I didn't return to class that period but stayed in the stall and cried until the bell rang. I ate lunch with Addison, but Loxley was in the other building. The elementary kids were kept separate from the rest of us. They played separately, learned separately and ate separately. Knowing Loxley, she was having a fine old time. She was never one to go without a friend for too long, and I suspected that the smaller children were not as curious about Jeopardy's disappearance as were my own schoolmates. It was so strange that nobody mentioned her name. Actually, no one spoke to me much at all. It wasn't until after lunch that Arnette Loper came walking beside me. Jeopardy used to call her frog-face behind her back. She never cared for Arnette too much.

"I've been meaning to tell you for weeks, I'm so happy for you that you got voted into the Harvest Queen Court. And you looked real pretty at the dance, too. Of course, I'm sorry I didn't make it on the Court, but maybe next year. Older girls have a better chance, they say. I can't wait." Arnette ran on and on and then finally saw the sadness in my face as I remembered the night my sister disappeared. She said, "I'm real sorry about your sister. Jeopardy was..."

I stopped in the hallway, ignoring the impatient crowd behind me. They could walk around. "You mean Jeopardy *is*, Arnette. She's not dead. She's just missing."

"Oh, I didn't mean to imply that she was dead. Sorry, Harper." She clutched her notebook to her chest and looked up at me. I was a full three inches taller than Arnette; I was probably the tallest girl in the ninth grade.

Her voice dropped to a whisper, "Is it true that she ran off with a carnie? You know, the good-looking one who looked like Dean Martin. What was his name?"

"What are you talking about, Arnette? Jeopardy didn't run off with anyone. She's just missing." We started to move toward our biology class. The bell would ring soon, and I was glad because I really wanted to get away from Arnette.

"Well, Harper, she can't just be missing. She's got to be missing on purpose. I mean, someone would have to be taking care of her, right? It makes sense that she went off to get married, and that would be so like Jeopardy Belle. She was nothing if not romantic."

I hadn't thought about that before, and it certainly was a possibility, but a carnival worker? No way. If Jeopardy was gonna run off with anyone, it would've been with Troy Harvester. And where was Troy? His brother Tony held court in front of his locker before last period, but I hadn't seen Troy in a while. It was like he'd disappeared too.

"Anyway, I'm real sorry." She walked away and found a seat at the front of the class while I chose one at the back. Last year, I would've been right up front with Arnette, but not this year. I wanted to be as far from the spotlight as possible, plus she'd given me a lot to think about. What if it was true? What if Jeopardy did leave me behind? Would she have done that? I shook my head as I opened my notebook and prepared for the long boring biology speech I was sure Mr. Dempsey was about to give us. Mr. Dempsey might be dreamy, according to Arnette, but he loved nothing better than to talk on and on about nuclei and cells and other boring things. As he talked, I pretended people weren't looking back and staring at me like they'd done for weeks. I avoided their eyes and wrote Jeopardy's name about a hundred times before the class ended. I'd never been so glad to be out of school before, but every day without Jeopardy was just awful.

Arnette caught me in the classroom doorway. "Hey, why don't you ride with us? We're going to Lucedale to the soda shop."

"Hey, Harper," a boy with a shiny round face and cropped blond hair said with a nervous smile. I'd seen him before but couldn't recall ever speaking to him. He didn't say anything to Arnette, who merely stared at him with her bulging green eyes. The boy didn't shuffle away but stood with us as if he'd been a part of the conversation from the beginning.

"Um, hello. Benjamin, right?"

"Only Dempsey calls me that. I'm Ben or Benny. Hartley." He was sweating pretty good but extended his hand to Arnette. She shook it.

"Benny, I was just telling Harper that some of us were going for a soda after school. You game?"

"Sure," he said with a grin as he pulled his book strap up on his shoulder. "I've got a car. I'll be glad to drive you, Harper. And you..."

"Arnette," she said with an amused smile.

I shook my head. "No, thank you. I appreciate the offer, but I'd better go home. I think my grandfather is picking me up." Arnette smiled good-naturedly, and I instantly liked her again. I know she didn't mean to hurt my feelings or insinuate that Jeopardy was some kind of fast girl. Arnette was just being Arnette. Benny looked disappointed, but I gave him a polite finger wave and he perked back up.

"Goodbye, Harper."

"Ciao," Arnette called after him. That was her new thing. She'd seen it in some movie with Ava Gardner or some glamorous star like that. When was the last time I had been to the movies? I glanced back one more time at Benny. Nope. Still didn't recall him.

Addison waited for me at the front door, and together we walked out into the sunshine.

"Who was that boy?" she asked between sneezes.

"Just a friend." I handed her my one and only hand-kerchief. I dreaded the ride home. I didn't like my grandfather at all, and it seemed strange to me that he would want to be a part of our lives now that Daddy and Jeopardy were gone. We stood outside, and Loxley ran toward us holding up a piece of paper. In class today, she got to glue macaroni onto paper. Before I had the opportunity to compliment her on her artwork, a horn honked. To my sheer joy, I saw Aunt Dot sitting in her convertible. She waved at us and called my name.

We all ran toward her. Maybe today wouldn't be so bad after all. Maybe it would end with some laughter and happiness. Aunt Dot always brought sunshine with her. We hopped in the car as she drove away, and I pretended that I didn't see my grandfather's Master DeLuxe just four cars back. He honked at us, but none of us paid attention. Addison finally looked back and tapped me on the shoulder, but I touched my finger to my lips to encourage her to keep quiet. She nodded back with wide eyes. Loxley had taken the front seat today, but Addison and I didn't complain.

For the first time in a long time, I felt joy. Real joy. It wouldn't last long.

# *Chapter Five—Jerica*

I woke up feeling groggy, but then again, I'd stayed up much later than I normally would. Since leaving the third shift at the Sunrise Retirement Home behind, I'd gotten used to going to bed at a decent hour. Despite last evening's frightening beginnings, my date with Jesse went well. Instead of going to the new steakhouse, we drove through the Sonic, ordered a bunch of junk food and went back to his place. Nothing intimate happened beyond some handholding on his front porch swing, but it had been a nice evening, especially after the terror we experienced at Summerleigh. For the first time in a long time, my first thought of the morning was not imagining the arms of my daughter around my neck or the sound of her footsteps running to my bed. I felt a tad guilty about that but whispered, "Good morning, Marisol," as I always did. I listened quietly for a response, knowing that there would be none. The only sound I heard was a bird fussing in the live oak outside my window.

As I waited for the fog to lift, I recalled with perfect clarity the strange little boy Jesse and I saw standing in the hallway of Summerleigh last night. We had talked for hours about it but were no closer to understanding what forces were at work. The little boy was clearly not a Belle; we assumed he was a member of the McIntyre family, but since that was so long ago, we had no real way of identifying him. One thing was for sure, though—whoever or whatever he was did not like the repairs and improvements we were making. I rolled over and stared at the clock. It was already eight, and Hannah was scheduled to be here at nine. The hard work of the past week left me feeling tired and sore, but it felt good. I'd forgotten how much I loved working with my hands and the pure exhaustion that came with intense physical labor. I used to save lives, and now I saved houses.

Or at least I was trying to save the house. I wondered if I should have so readily ignored Ben Hartley's warning. Maybe I shouldn't stay. But how could I just leave? This place felt like home, and Marisol had followed me here. What if I left and she didn't come with me?

*Maybe I'll call Ben today and insist that he tell me what he knows. Maybe he's seen the boy too. Yeah, that's what I'll do,* I promised myself.

The hour flew by, and Hannah knocked on my door promptly at nine. "Good morning. Come in," I greeted her with a smile.

Hannah was tall, taller than most, and she seemed really self-conscious about that. As always, she clutched her purse close to her like a life vest. She didn't appear nervous or frightened as she had been when she called last night.

"Would you like something to drink? Maybe a cup of coffee?" I asked as I led her into the kitchen.

She politely declined and took a seat at the table. "You went to Summerleigh, didn't you?"

I finished pouring my own cup of coffee and took a seat across from her. I smoothed out the tablecloth and shrugged. "I had no intention of going over there, but after you called, I—I mean, we—saw a light in the attic. Jesse was here. And since we had equipment and materials in the house, we couldn't ignore it. How did you know that there would be activity?"

Still clutching her purse, Hannah tilted her head and looked past me thoughtfully as if trying to figure out how to best answer my question. "Ever since I visited Summerleigh, the energy there has kind of stayed with me. It's like I have this weird connection with it now. That happens sometimes; it's a risk that psychics take, and it usually doesn't amount to anything, but this time was different. I'm always careful, but I left Summerleigh with a heaviness, an attachment for lack of a better word. I'm positive it originated from something in that house. My alarm bells went off, and I couldn't stop thinking about Summerleigh. When I saw your daughter, it kind of clicked. I think she came to warn me."

"Marisol? You saw my daughter?"

"Yes. She was worried about you, Jerica. I think she's trying to protect you."

Tears filled my eyes, but I blinked them back. Hannah offered me a tissue from her purse. I dabbed at my face as she continued, "I'm not like a lot of psychic mediums, meaning that I don't commune with spirits the way some psychics do. I sense energy more than anything, not usually ghosts directly, so that's why it surprised me to see Marisol and get those impressions about the house. I can sense when energy builds and dissipates. Right now, I know energy is building. The spirit world is stirred up, and there are many eyes concentrated on this place. How about you? Are you feeling anything unusual? You have a rare sensitivity, Jerica. I think that's why Harper picked you."

"I've had a few things happen, but I didn't think much of them because Jeopardy Belle has been found. We recovered her remains."

"But Harper...you still see Harper," Hannah said wide-eyed. It wasn't really a question.

"Yes. I have dreamed about Harper a few times recently. Her grandfather, the man who murdered Jeopardy, is coming around again. But if he'd done anything to Harper, I would've known about it. She would have told me. We were friends, and if she suspected he had anything to do with Jeopardy..."

Hannah reached across the table and held my hand. "When you're dealing with the supernatural, it's really important that you don't assume anything. I know that's hard when your emotions are involved, but it may be that Harper wants you to know something. Something that will help you." She patted my hand one last time and sat up straight. "I think we should take a walk, Jerica. Let's go check out the house."

"I don't want to put you in further danger, Hannah."

"It's the only way I can help you, and I have my protection now. I have no one to blame but myself for that last incident. I know better than to walk into a place like Summerleigh without preparing. Lesson learned. Let's go check it out. Unless you want me to go by myself?"

"No way. You should know that Jesse and I both saw the boy with the black eyes last night. He was on the top floor, and I got the distinct impression that he did not want us there." We rose from the table, and I put my cup in the sink. I locked the back door, and we stepped out the front into the warm sunshine. I hadn't noticed how chilly it had become in the cottage.

"Tell me what happened, and don't leave anything out," she prompted me as she pulled her purse higher up on her shoulder.

"Jesse and I were in the kitchen, and we saw a light moving in the attic. It wasn't like a flashlight beam, more like a strange disco light. There were different colors; first white and then blue and purple and then white again. And it moved around, so it kind of looked like someone was having a party in the attic. I told Jesse what you said about not going in the house, but like I said, we couldn't ignore it." I closed the front door behind me and locked it before we walked down the gravel path toward the front door of Summerleigh. I could avoid going through the back door in the daylight.

"And?"

"We heard what sounded like a child's footsteps, so we went up to check it out. When we got to the end of the hallway on the second floor, we could see the light shining under the door, and you could see the shadows of someone passing through it. While we were busy trying to open the door, the boy appeared at the end of the hall. The doors started slamming—I mean they were slamming so hard it sounded like they were going to be ripped off the hinges. I won't lie; I was scared out of my mind. I don't know what I would have done without Jesse. The sound kept getting louder and louder." I put the key in the door of Summerleigh and turned it slowly. "I couldn't take it anymore, so I screamed. I said, 'Quit it!' or something like that, and it all stopped. Jesse and I didn't waste any time getting out of there."

"Interesting. He listened to you. He must know that this is your place now. Still, I can't imagine he'll go without a fight."

We stepped inside the Great Room. I left the door open because the air was so heavy that it felt like it might smother me. "I almost forgot, Jerica. I made this for you." Hannah dug inside her purse and retrieved a necklace. After untangling the chain, she handed it to me. It was a silver chain with an odd blue pendant. "This will protect you while we're here. Let's go upstairs to the center of the activity. Funny, though, I don't feel any of the Belles in here. Not even John, the father."

As we walked toward the staircase, I sighed sadly. All of the happiness and goodwill that I felt earlier this week, all the hard work we put into restoring Summerleigh, seemed so worthless now. Perhaps Ben Hartley was right. This place was cursed.

"Oh yes. The boy is here. Such an unhappy entity. Definitely human, so at least there are limitations to his power. But I get the sense that he is..." Hannah paused on the stairs and looked behind her.

"What? What is it?"

"It's just a voice, a droning in my ear. Don't you hear it?"

I shook my head but listened for a minute. The hair all over my body crept up. "Let's keep going. I'll see if I can communicate with the boy, but if he's anything like last time, I'm not sure how successful I'll be. If we can figure out what he wants, maybe we can help him move on."

I remembered something important from a dream I had recently. "I forgot to tell you, Hannah. Loxley, the youngest Belle girl, admitted to Harper that she was the one who cut up her dress with the scissors. She said the boy wanted her to do it...and in fact, he was the one who gave her the scissors. And I remember Jesse mentioned once before that Mariana McIntyre was murdered with a pair of scissors. I'm not sure if that means anything, but I figured I'd tell you."

Hannah nodded as she clutched her purse and whispered to herself. With nervous hands, she removed a small electronic device from her pocket. She clicked the button, paused on the top stair and then slowly began to move down the hall, looking through each open doorway as she went. I followed a few steps behind her.

*Was she praying? Maybe I should pray too?*

Hannah said, "Little boy, I know you are here. We're not here to harm you, but you cannot harm us either. We need to know, are you a McIntyre? Was Mariana your sister?" She waved her recorder around and then walked into the room that the Belle girls always referred to as the nursery. It was as silent as the grave. We waited but heard nothing except the sound of scurrying somewhere. *Oh great, please don't let there be mice in here.*

"Oh yes, you like it in here, don't you? This was your own little kingdom, wasn't it?" I heard a bumping sound coming from the nearby closet, but Hannah didn't react to it. She continued to walk around the room and finally put her device in the window. "This lady owns this house now. This is not your house anymore. There are no children here for you to play with. You should go, be with your family." Another bumping sound came from the closet, and I was feeling less comfortable by the second. "Why are you hiding from us? I'm not opening that closet door. We're not playing with you. You need to leave." The door handle on the closet began to shake as if an invisible hand tugged on it. I stepped back and stood in the corner of the room, my pulse racing and my hands sweating. Hannah extended her hand behind her and waved at me to calm me down. I tried to keep cool, but it wasn't working. She waved at me again and looked back at me, lifting her chin to prompt me to speak.

"My name is Jerica Poole. Summerleigh is mine now. I don't want you here." The door to the closet flung open, but there was nothing inside. Not a strange boy with a hateful stare. No lady in white. Not even a coat hanger. All I could see was a dust-covered floor.

Hannah stepped up beside me. "Let's go, Jerica." As she went to retrieve the device from the window, it flew across the room and smashed against the opposite wall. I shrieked and did a side step, but Hannah didn't flinch. We both raced over to examine the damage. Hannah retrieved the batteries that had flown out the back. It didn't look like anything else was wrong with the machine. She popped the batteries back in, slid the back on and turned on the power. "It's still working," she said to me with a frown. Then she said loudly, "That was not very nice. We're leaving this room, and you cannot follow us. Remember, we are protected." Hannah made the sign of the cross, and I did the same. We walked out of the room, leaving the bone-chilling cold behind.

"You okay?" she asked as she patted my shoulder.

"Yeah. Just startled me."

"Let's head toward the attic. I think we should leave him alone."

"Does that happen a lot?"

"Some ghosts are intelligent, meaning they know what's happening. They may not understand that they are dead or that they exist in a different time, but they are intelligent nonetheless. I've found that most are not mean, but some are. I have the feeling that if we could ever discover his name, it would help us. He respects you, for some reason."

I whispered to her, "Is this other one, Mariana, intelligent also?"

"I'm not sure yet. She's intelligent enough to want to avoid us, but she might tell us what we need to know. There is certainly a residual aspect to her haunting, meaning she does the same thing over and over. She likes visiting the same places; she feels at home." We walked to the attic, and to my surprise, Hannah stopped and knocked softly on the door.

"Mariana? My name is Hannah Ray. My friend Jerica is with me. May we come in?" I reached for the doorknob, but Hannah touched my shoulder. "No. We can't go in." She stepped back and stared at the door.

"What? Why?"

"Let's leave. I think I need some air."

"Okay," I said as we walked back down the hall. I purposely did not look into the nursery as we passed by. I hurried down the stairs probably quicker than I should have and nearly tripped on the last step, but Hannah caught me. "Thanks." We walked outside, and I locked the door behind us. It felt good to stand in the sunshine. Hannah began to walk away from the house, and I caught up with her.

"Nothing can follow us. No one can follow us."

*Okay, that's worrying.* "It's not good, is it?"

"I'm going to go home and review this recorder to see if there are any clues as to who this child is, if he is a child."

"What do you mean if? I saw him. It was a boy."

Hannah shook her head and said, "Some very intelligent entities like putting on faces that are useful to them. If there were children in this house, it would make sense that he would appear to them as a child. Or if there is a mother missing her child..."

My heart sank. "Oh, I see." I rubbed my lip with my finger. "But you said that it was definitely a human."

"Yes, but it may not be a boy. It could be a man or a woman. Who knows?"

"I have to know, Hannah. Why did you stop me from going into the attic?"

"I'm not sure. It just felt like the wrong time to go in. I'm sorry, Jerica. I don't mean to sound so mysterious, and I wish there were more I could tell you. It's just not how things work. Summerleigh is a very active place, and although most of the Belles appear to be at rest, there are other spirits here. They need to be dealt with too. I'd like to come back and bring a few friends with me. People with similar gifts who know more than I do."

I sighed and tried to fight the frustration that threatened to overwhelm me. "My crew is coming back Monday, so tomorrow would be okay."

"Tomorrow it is, then. I'll call you with the details as soon as I hear from my friends. In the meantime, Jerica, go for a walk. Spend some time outdoors. That's where you'll find your strength. And stay out of Summerleigh. I don't care how many lights you see. Don't go in there by yourself." Hannah paused on the pathway before getting into her car.

I wrapped my arms around myself, suddenly feeling very alone.

"You haven't asked me about her."

"I know she's here. That's enough for now." The truth was I wasn't ready to say goodbye to Marisol. And for some reason, I believed that if I did truly connect with her, I'd never see her again. Ever.

Hannah closed the door and rolled the window down. "When you're ready, just ask." Then she drove away.

I brushed a tear from my eye and decided not to wait for that walk. As my father used to say, "There's no time like the present." I stuffed my cold hands in my pockets and kicked a rock in my path. With a glance at the looming mansion behind me, I turned away from the house and tried to ignore the feeling of eyes watching me.

I didn't shake the feeling until I reached the river.

## *Chapter Six—Harper*

I pleaded with Aunt Dot to let us stay the night at her house, but I didn't quite come out and explain why. What would I say? *Mr. Daughdrill makes Momma cry and wants me to call him Grandfather now. Like Jeopardy used to.* As always, my sunny aunt didn't want to hear anything negative about her sister, but then again, Aunt Dot was a glass-is-half-full kind of gal. Even though we couldn't stay the night, she did take us shopping; I didn't get the exact outfit that I saw in the magazine, but Aunt Dot bought me three scarves and two new skirts. Addison and Loxley got new dresses and shoes. With a trunk full of packages, we headed down Highway 98 back home to Desire.

The closer we got to Hurlette Drive, the more Addison rubbed her stomach and the whinier Loxley became. Couldn't Aunt Dot see how upset we were?

"Let's sing a driving song," she said to me with a big smile in the rearview mirror. I wanted to smile back but didn't have the energy to summon one. "The wheels on the bus go round and round, round and round, round and round." Nobody joined in. Aunt Dot's smile disappeared, and for the first time, I understood that my aunt was nervous too. She didn't want to leave us at Summerleigh any more than we wanted to go.

With a sigh, she eased into the slow lane and said, "Girls, you know I would take you all home with me if I could. But I can't. What about your Momma? She's a handful at times, but she has a good heart. I know she's moody and unreasonable, Harper, but you have to remember she's lost a husband. And with Jeopardy being gone, Ann is a broken soul, and we've all got to be patient with her."

I didn't bother answering her; she'd made up her mind not to see the bad things. Not to know that we were hungry and hurting. She didn't want to see how completely abandoned we all felt. It was easier that way, I guessed. Still, despite her naivety—I never believed I'd ever use one of my vocabulary words in a sentence—I didn't hate her. One could only love sweet Aunt Dot. I gazed out the window at the trees as we rushed past them. The shadows were gathering, and it would be time for supper soon. I wondered what I'd find in the refrigerator, if anything. There were some jars of tomatoes in the pantry. Maybe I could whip up some tomato gravy and biscuits. We had flour; I knew we had flour.

"Harper, are you listening, dear?"

"Yes, Aunt Dot," I lied as she talked about how things were going to get better, how things would turn around for us Belle girls. She wasn't fooling anyone in the car. Except maybe Loxley, who joined her in singing "When We All Get to Heaven."

"How about I pick you girls up for church on Sunday, if your Momma is still too ill to go? You haven't been in almost a month of Sundays." She chuckled as if she'd made the biggest joke ever. I didn't have the energy now to appease her determined sense of humor. I suddenly remembered that I wasn't wearing my hose. I'd stuffed them in my purse at school and forgot to put them back on. I hoped Momma didn't notice. It would be bad if she did.

"That would be fine, Aunt Dot." Addison glanced back at me as if she were expecting me to say something too. I couldn't. I was too busy counting. The car turned down the drive. I counted the seconds from the turn. It was twenty seconds from that turn until the first glimpse of Summerleigh. As we got closer, I felt sicker. Despite the presents and the renewed friendship with Arnette Loper, I wasn't any happier than I had been when I left home this morning. Funny how I'd almost become accustomed to the gloom that had fallen on Summerleigh, how differently I felt about the place now that Daddy would never return to bring her back to life. And I missed Jeopardy with all my heart.

Momma wasn't alone at the house. Thankfully, Mr. Daughdrill's car wasn't there, but a rusty red truck sat in the driveway. Aunt Dot's car crept to a stop, and she turned off the radio. She slid the gearshift into park and stared at the vehicle and then at the brightly lit parlor. *Wait a minute. I recognize that truck.* It belonged to Dewey Landry, Aunt Dot's sometime sweetheart! The curtains were open, and I could see Momma and the dark-haired man sitting on the couch together. Momma's legs were curled up under her dress, and she was smoking and laughing like everything was hunky-dory.

"Who is that? I can't see his face," Addison said to no one in particular.

I knew, and apparently so did Aunt Dot. She didn't take her eyes off the window, and all four of us watched as Momma whispered in Dewey's ear and he slapped his knee at her joke. I was completely shocked. Jeopardy had always claimed that Momma had "friends" coming to the house at late hours, but I'd never seen one myself. It wasn't that late now, but it was Dewey Landry. What was she thinking? With his slicked-back brown hair, plain white t-shirt and blue jeans, Dewey was practically naked in our parlor. I didn't know which I found more troubling, Momma entertaining Dewey like she was a teenage girl and he her high school crush or my aunt's teary-eyed expression.

Aunt Dot opened the car door. "You girls stay here. I'll be right back."

"Yes, Aunt Dot," we said in unison. Count Basie blared from the radio in the parlor, and Momma's laughter escalated like it always did after she'd had a few drinks. I knew this song, "Take Me Back, Baby." We weren't allowed to listen to it at home, but the kids at school loved it. Tony Harvester liked playing Basie as loud as he could on his car radio. For the hundredth time today, I thought of Jeopardy. What would she think about seeing Momma in the house with a man who wasn't Daddy? *I told you so, Harper. Momma ain't nothing but a w-h-o-r-e. Wait until I tell Daddy.*

"Harper? I'm afraid," Loxley whined as she poked her head over the back seat for a better view.

"That's Dewey Landry," Addison declared finally. "What's he doing here?"

"Maybe he's here to fix the refrigerator. He is a repairman," I lied to my little sister too easily. Addison sneezed again in the front seat. I watched in horror as Aunt Dot cleared the distance between the car and the house and walked right into the parlor. Clearly, she was yelling at Momma and Dewey, but I couldn't hear her over the radio. Like a cornered wildcat, Momma sprang to her feet and threw her glass on the floor. I'd have to clean that up, and the carpet. And then Dewey was up, his hands in front of him as if he believed he'd be able to control the situation. What a fool he was to think he'd be able to calm those two. Next thing I knew, Aunt Dot and Momma were tussling. I couldn't tell who threw the first punch because Dewey blocked my vision. He was still trying to break them up.

"We have to stop them, Harper!" Addison was out of the car without waiting for an answer. Loxley began to cry beside me, and I held her, still too shocked to move. Seeing Addison running through the yard clutching her stomach stirred me—I couldn't just sit here like a bump on a log and let her get hurt. That's when I saw another car roll up behind me. I knew the shape of the headlights immediately. This was none other than Mr. Daughdrill in his Chevy Master DeLuxe.

"Holy smokes," I said as I tried to sink down in the car. I don't know why I tried; it was impossible to hide from those lights, which shone like two white suns. Mr. Daughdrill wasted no time running to the porch and ordering Addison to stay outside. He stepped inside just in time to see Aunt Dot slap Dewey across the face as Momma collapsed on her red velvet sofa in a crying heap. In a few steps, Mr. Daughdrill crossed the room and unplugged the radio, then slung Dewey Landry out of the house. Both of his daughters stood up and faced him, screaming words we weren't allowed to say, being Baptists and all. Then Mr. Daughdrill struck Momma across the face, and she hit the ground. He grabbed her by her blond hair, just like she'd done to me, and struck her again. I had never seen such violence. Aunt Dot crumpled back, obviously too frightened to intervene.

Before I knew it, I was screaming, "Momma!" I ran to the house with Loxley in my arms. I don't know how I managed to climb out of that back seat holding her, but I did it. She'd peed on me as she cried, but I couldn't stop and change her clothing. Addison trailed behind me as we raced inside. Loxley was weeping loudly, and she ran to Aunt Dot as soon as she saw her.

From some place unseen and unknown within me, anger exploded and I yelled at Mr. Daughdrill, "Don't you ever hit her again!" I picked up the poker from the fireplace and held it in my hand. I was no small girl, and I had quite an arm on me. He might be six inches taller, but I would strike him as sure as I was standing here if he hit Momma again. "Get out of our house now! Get out of here, you mean old bastard!" I'd never used that word before, and it shocked everyone into silence. Except Aunt Dot.

"Harper Louise," she said in a steady, quiet voice, "Put the poker down. It's all over now."

"Girl, don't you ever threaten me again. I see now what a horrible mother you are, Ann. Here you are, rollicking like a harlot with a two-bit grease monkey, and now your children disrespect me. I will not tolerate this any longer. There will be order." He grabbed Addison's arm—for what intention, I did not know, but his words broke me. That was the last thing Mr. Daughdrill said to me because I struck him hard across the opposite arm. He let go of Addison, who scrambled to Aunt Dot. Every feeling I had, all the grief and sadness, exploded into uncontrollable anger, and I struck him not once or twice but at least a half-dozen times.

And nobody moved to stop me.

"That's enough now, Harper," Momma said in a whisper. She lifted her bruised face to me. I couldn't discern her expression. Was it relief? Anger?

My hands stung, and I could see that I'd bruised them. I dropped the poker. It landed on the carpet with a thud, and I backed away from the sight of Mr. Daughdrill bleeding on the parlor floor.

"Look, he's breathing," Addison said as she craned her neck to see him.

"Girls, get in the car. We're leaving," Aunt Dot whispered as she held Loxley tighter.

Momma began to cry, but she didn't argue about it. I don't think she was crying because we were leaving.

I felt sure she was crying because I almost killed her daddy. Or something. Or maybe she was crying because we saw her fooling around with Dewey. I couldn't be sure. Whatever the reason, I couldn't leave her alone. Not now.

"I can't go, Aunt Dot. I have to stay and take care of Momma," I said in a wooden voice. I couldn't believe my own ears. What was I saying? I'd been praying for weeks—no, months—to get away from Momma, to leave Summerleigh forever. Now here was my chance and I couldn't do it.

Aunt Dot's mascara ran beneath her eyes, and her hat was crooked from the earlier melee. "No, you don't have to stay. I'm sorry I didn't listen before. Come with me, Harper Louise. I won't let you go through this another day."

With all my heart, I wanted to leave with her. I wanted to burn Summerleigh to the ground, along with every sad memory I had of this place, but I couldn't leave Momma. She'd have no one if I left. No one at all.

"I'm sorry, Aunt Dot. I can't go." To my surprise, Addison took my hand. She didn't speak, but I squeezed it back.

"All right," Aunt Dot said sadly. "Ann, I'm leaving with Loxley. I'll make sure she gets to school."

Momma nodded and reached out her hand to me. Her beautiful face was the picture of sadness, as if all her hopes were now pinned on me. Aunt Dot and

Loxley left, and I heard the car pull out of the driveway.

The blood around Mr. Daughdrill pooled, but he was still breathing.

I took Momma's hand and helped her to her feet. She fell on my shoulder and cried like I was her best friend, but I knew better than that.

I wasn't her friend. I was her prisoner.

## *Chapter Seven—Jerica*

John Jeffrey Belle had been right. The pond was nothing more than a glorified mud hole except for a few ducks that called it home. I walked farther, deciding that I would go down to Dog River and look at the water there. Jeopardy Belle used to love going down to Dog River. I remembered Troy Harvester's description of her rising out of the water "like some kind of siren." I wanted to see it for myself again. I'd been down there once before and had seen my daughter briefly. She'd been playing with Loxley Belle. In retrospect, I think Marisol wanted me to know that she was happy here at Summerleigh. She liked that I was here, but now I wasn't so sure. I didn't feel her like I used to. I didn't see her, and I couldn't understand why she was being so elusive.

And then it dawned on me. Maybe the boy with the black eyes forced her to leave Summerleigh. Maybe he was keeping her away from me. Maybe he wanted to keep me all to himself. Yes, that could be it. Marisol was scared and hiding from him. All the more reason to get rid of him.

"Marisol, honey," I said with my eyes closed and my face turned up to the sun, "I'll never let anything happen to you. Never again. I failed you once before, my baby, but I'll never do it again. Trust Momma, please. Can you hear me?"

Then as clear as a bell I heard a splash in the water. Not a fish jumping or a pebble plunking into the water but a splash as if someone had jumped in. I twisted around on the rock and looked over in the water just in time to see a spray of bubbles appear. I waited and waited, but nobody emerged from the murky water. I looked around and stood up on the rock to see if I could locate anyone near me. I searched for any evidence that someone was down here on this part of Dog River besides me but couldn't see a soul. Scanning the banks again, I checked for clothing or a boat but saw no one. And then the water stopped bubbling, the ripples ceased to move, and it was as if it never happened.

*I know that just happened. I know someone dived in. I heard it with my own two ears. Oh, God! What if he was in trouble?*

Without taking off my shoes or emptying my pockets, I dived in. Fear and urgency overwhelmed me. I swam with all my might, and when I got to the spot that I believed I'd seen the splash, I dived down in a panic.

Beneath the surface, the water wasn't as murky as I expected, but it was much deeper than I had believed. Under the top layer of brown water, the bottom part of the river was clean and crystal-clear and fast moving. I swam about, looking for someone, anyone to rescue. I was running out of air, so I swam quickly back to the surface and sucked in a breath, then dived again and swam down a few feet. For one fleeting moment, I thought I saw a figure, but then it was gone. Someone *was* down here! My lungs burned, and I breached the surface again to catch my breath. I had every intention of diving back down until I saw a man standing on the shore.

The sun was behind him, so I couldn't see his face clearly. "Hey! Help! I think someone is drowning," I shouted. An icy-cold chill passed over me, and I slunk down in the water a bit. I peered hard at the man, but he didn't seem to hear me.

*Oh no. I know who he is, but that can't be possible!* It was Mr. Daughdrill, Harper's long-dead grandfather! I raised my hand to my eyes to shield them from the sun, but I still could not see his face. I had no desire to swim to shore and see the ghost face-to-face. *What do I do? I can't swim to the shore as long as he's standing there. How is this possible?* Treading water furiously now, I thought about my options. I could swim downstream and then find another way home. Or I could stay in the water until someone else showed up. Surely someone else would come.

"Marisol!" I whispered. "Stay away." The man didn't move. The wind blew, but his hair and clothing did not. He wore the same loose gray suit that I'd seen him in before, in Harper's memories. Yes, that was Daughdrill. Who else could it be?

And that's when I felt the tug on my foot. A strong tug. I screamed in surprise and tried to swim away. That was not a branch or a piece of debris—that was a hand grabbing me! I screamed, but the scream was choked out with water as I was plunged beneath the surface of the suddenly violent waves. *Let me go!* I tried to yell, but no one could hear me. I thought I would drown as the hand gripped my ankle tighter. The last thing I wanted to do was see who or what had me, but I had no choice other than to swim down. I had to get free! With my last bit of oxygen, I released a bit of air and dived down to face the bloated white face that met mine.

This was the boy with the black eyes, the one from Summerleigh!

He was here in the water, and he wanted to drown me. He wanted me to die. I kicked at him so hard with my other foot that I felt his slippery skin move beneath my foot. I gagged at the sight of pieces of his flesh floating away in the water. He let me go and disappeared as he fell down further into the river. I launched to the surface, breathing in air as quickly as possible. A scream erupted from my lips, and I swam to the other side of the river, screaming and crying all the way. I had to get away from the boy. I prayed as I swam. Looking over my shoulder once or twice, I realized that no one was there. Daughdrill was gone.

I eased up on the muddy bank of Dog River and held my ankle in my hand. It was clearly bruised but not broken. I was a nurse after all; I knew what breaks looked like. I got up on my feet as quickly as possible—I had to get away from this hellish river.

I thought I would have a peaceful day out here, spend some time in nature and get away from the ghosts of the house. Maybe see Marisol again. Unfortunately, the ghosts had come looking for me.

Hannah was wrong. I was not protected, and the boy with the black eyes was not going away easily. And he had an evil friend. I left immediately and began walking along the opposite bank until I came to a bridge that would lead me back to the other side of the river. The road was lonely, and I suddenly realized this was the road where Jeopardy had gone missing. This was the road where Daughdrill had done his last Horrible Thing—he took Jeopardy's life right here. I paused, feeling sick. I heard a car approaching but didn't stick around to see who it was. I hurried through the woods back to the cottage.

The sick feeling morphed into something else. I was angry. Angry that children had been hurt. Angry that Daughdrill thought he could harm me by sending that demented child after me.

*I understand now, Harper. I know what you want me to know. You were a fighter. You were never a quitter—you never gave up on Jeopardy or any of your family. Not even your Momma. I know this about you because you never gave up on me, either. And you knew that I'm like you. I am a fighter too, Harper.*

*And this isn't over yet.*

## *Chapter Eight—Harper*

For a long time, none of us said a word. After I helped Momma to her feet, she sat on the couch and stared at Mr. Daughdrill, who hadn't moved an inch. It was Addison who spoke first. "I think you killed him, Harper. I think he's dead for sure. Truly I do think it."

"No, he's not. I can see him breathing, Addie." I did see him breathing, didn't I? Or was I imagining that? I felt sick all of a sudden and panicked. "I'm sorry, Momma. I didn't mean to do it."

And then I heard him moaning and murmuring, "Ann, help me, girl. Ann..." His eyes were open, but he couldn't move his mouth. Had I broken his jaw?

Momma stiffened her back and sat up straight on the couch. She tucked her feet beneath her, posed as pretty as any picture, without making a move to help him. She stared down at her father, and we all watched him move his fingers. Yes, he was starting to move now. He might even be up and moving in a few minutes. She said, "Girls, you get cleaned up and get dressed for bed."

"Shouldn't we call a doctor or someone?" Addison asked in a small, scared voice.

Momma shook her head once and tilted it as if she were posing, just like one of her old photo shoots. All the tears and desperation I saw on her face had been replaced with something else. Something cold and calculating, something ladylike and calm. I think I would've rather had her tear my hair out than behave so calmly.

"You just leave everything to me, Addison," she said as she rose from the couch and smoothed her pencil skirt. Neither one of us girls moved. All we could do was stare at her. Had she lost her senses? We needed to call the police. I'd probably be arrested. "Do as Momma tells you now. Both of you."

In unison, we said, "Yes, Momma." Addison took my hand and led me out of the parlor, into the Great Room and into the hallway that led to our rooms. "Stay with me tonight, Harper. I can't sleep by myself."

"All right, Addie," I said as I sat on her bed and stared off into the distance. My body shook, my hands hurt, and I could see bruises on my fingers. I couldn't stop staring at them. These were proof that I had it too. I had the same rage Momma and her father had. Even Aunt Dot had it. I saw that tonight. Deep inside me, the Daughdrill rage had lain hidden all these years, but it was there. And now I would go to prison. People who kill people, people who beat people, they send them to prison. I'd probably die in prison.

Addie was talking to me, but I couldn't hear her. Then she put her hand under my chin and stared into my eyes. "Harper, can you hear me?"

"Yes, I hear you. I'm so tired, Addison. I just want to sleep."

"You heard Momma; we have to get ready for bed."

"I just want to lie down," I murmured, feeling so lightheaded I feared I might actually faint. My hands and head throbbed.

I lay on her pillow and drew my legs up to my chest. Without another word, Addison removed my shoes, covered me with her worn but heavy quilt and crept in beside me. I stared at the wall for a few minutes, but it didn't take long to fall asleep.

"It's all right, Harper Louise. I won't leave you. It's okay. Go to sleep now." Addison sniffled as she scooted up to my back.

I tried to say, "Thank you, Addie," but I found that I couldn't speak. I was too tired. I fell into a black, dreamless sleep.

I woke up feeling cold and realized that the quilt had been pulled off me. I reached behind me, thinking that Addison had stolen it in her sleep, but it wasn't there. The quilt was not on the bed. I sat up and looked for it. We must have kicked it off because it was lying on the floor at the foot of the bed.

*Get up, pie-face.*

I sat up in my bed straight as a board, like one of those old dolls whose back refused to bend because of age. "Jeopardy!"

*You coming or what?*

"Jeopardy Belle?" A smile stretched across my face because I knew that voice. Addison stirred beside me. She reached for me, but I was already on my feet. I heard Jeopardy's light steps traveling down the hall toward the Great Room.

"Harper? Where you going?"

"Come on, Addison. It's Jeopardy!"

"Really?" Addison was by my side now, and I held her hand as we hurried down the hall following Jeopardy's footsteps. This was a dream come true! Was I dreaming? I had dreamed so many times of Jeopardy's return. But I knew I was awake—I could feel the cold floor beneath my bare feet, and my lungs burned because the air all around me was cold. I glanced back and saw Addison's pale face. Her teeth were chattering.

I could hear Momma's radio playing in the parlor. It wasn't loud, not like earlier when she was entertaining Dewey Landry, but low and quiet. She was talking to someone, but who? Surely not Jeopardy. There was no love lost between those two. I paused to eavesdrop on her conversation. No, she was on the phone. I could tell by the tone of her voice. I wondered if I would see Mr. Daughdrill lying on the floor dead if I peeked into the parlor. There was no time to consider that. As we tiptoed through the near-empty Great Room to head up the stairs, I heard an odd sound. A thump. No, two thumps. Momma wasn't on the phone after all!

A man murmured in the other room. Was Dewey Landry back? Knowing that someone else might be in the house, I raced up the stairs with Addison in tow. We had to find Jeopardy and keep her out of sight. Way out of sight. I'd have to warm up Momma before I told her that Jeopardy had returned. Unlike Addison and Loxley and me, Momma had unpredictable moods. She might not be happy that Jeopardy had returned. But why? I'd never understand it.

And after what happened tonight, perhaps it was me Jeopardy should be afraid of. I nearly killed someone. But he wasn't dead, was he? Momma said he wasn't. I was sure he was hurt pretty bad, though. I forced the memory out of my mind, and Addison moaned behind me as she stubbed a toe on a worn step.

"Quiet," I whispered to her as we hurried up the last of the steps. We were on the second floor now, and if I thought it was cold downstairs, it felt like the freezer of the soda shop up here.

Addison hugged me and said, "Harper, I'm afraid. What are we doing up here?"

"I heard Jeopardy's voice, and so did you. Jeopardy is here." And then as if she were hurrying us along, the attic door slowly began to open. It squeaked on its hinges as it opened wide inch by inch, like Jeopardy was welcoming us inside her castle room. There was nothing but blackness in the attic, but I had to go on. I had to see Jeopardy Belle. I wanted to hold her in my arms and never let her go. My heart pounded as I thought about finally telling her how sorry I was that I had wrongly blamed her for destroying my dress. How sorry I was that I didn't do more for her. And if she wasn't happy at Summerleigh, we'd run away. The three of us. Jeopardy, Addison and me. We would leave Desire, Mississippi, behind and go explore the world. We were all smart and hard-working. We could make our way in the world.

"Come on, Addison," I said, smiling back at her as we raced to the attic.

*But what about Loxley?* I argued with myself. Addison whined again. What was the matter with her? We stood in the doorway now, peeking inside.

"Jeopardy Belle, where are you?"

She didn't answer, but I could sense that she was watching us from the darkness. "Come on, Addie." I hurried into the cluttered room. It wasn't as cold in here, and Jeopardy had been kind enough to light a candle. It wasn't much of a candle, only a few inches of white stub, but it was enough to illuminate her makeshift bed. I laughed to see it.

"Jeopardy? Why are you hiding? Come out this instant." I laughed at her playfulness. But then Jeopardy did not emerge from the shadows. Addie clutched my hands and stood in front of me. She put her pale face near mine. I didn't realize until that moment how tall she'd gotten; she was almost my height, and I was nearly as tall as Momma.

"Harper Louise, we can't stay here. Jeopardy isn't here. You were dreaming."

Dumbfounded, I blinked at her. I didn't dream any of this. I heard Jeopardy! She called me pie-face. "I didn't dream that candle, Addison. I didn't dream her voice; I know it like I know yours. It was her, all right. She's here, but she's being ridiculous. Jeopardy, if you don't come out right now, I'm going back downstairs. I mean it." I waited. Still nothing. "All right, you give me no choice. I'm counting to three—no more games. One...two..."

At the far side of the room where the junk was stacked the tallest, where there were trunks and crates arranged haphazardly on top of one another, I saw Jeopardy. But only for the briefest of seconds. It was as if a shaft of moonlight had hit her, revealing her hiding spot to me. She still wore those clunky white shoes, the one she'd taken from Momma. Her wild hair was around her shoulders, and she looked as pale as a sheet of paper. She even had her purse on her shoulder, which I knew was impossible. The sheriff's deputy had brought the shoes and purse to us the day they found them. Then she vanished. There was no more light, except for the candle.

And then I knew the horrible truth.

Wherever she was, Jeopardy was never coming home. I hadn't seen her at all, not living and breathing Jeopardy Belle. This was not her, just her shadow. Wild and brave Jeopardy was gone forever, and I'd seen her ghost. Addison saw her too because she was crying now. And then as quickly as I understood the horribleness of it all, I felt myself falling.

I welcomed the darkness.

# *Chapter Nine—Jerica*

To my dismay, Hannah's phone went directly to voicemail. I hoped that meant she was communicating with her paranormal investigator friends and trying to pull together a few who might help me clear Summerleigh of its unwanted residents. The events of this morning left me feeling desperate, and I never wanted to swim in Dog River—or any other river—ever again. I left Hannah a message about my encounter at the river and immediately called Jesse.

"Hey. You busy?" I asked.

He paused, and I feared that he'd say yes, but he didn't. "Let me set this down." I heard a thud, and then he said, "What's going on?"

I paced the floor, twisting a strand of hair in my hand as I talked. How would I say this without sounding like a lunatic? "Do you think the boy and Mr. Daughdrill are connected somehow?"

"What? I don't think so. The McIntyre family was gone from Summerleigh in the 1870s, and the house was vacant for a long time before it was sold again. It wasn't until John Belle won it that Daughdrill came around. He wasn't hurting for money. The man owned several homes and hundreds of acres. Why?"

I plopped down on the couch and sighed. "You're not going to believe what happened to me this morning." I told him everything. Jesse knew there were ghosts at Summerleigh, but they were different now. It seemed they weren't limited to the house but were stalking me around the property.

I could hear the worry in his voice. "That's not good, Jerica. That's not good at all. Listen, I know this might sound inappropriate, but I really wish you'd spend the night here tonight. I've got the guest room, and I wouldn't mind the company. I could use a skilled helper. This boat isn't going to build itself."

I smiled at that. It did sound like fun, and I'd never worked on a boat before. But the nagging feeling that I shouldn't go was strong. I glanced around my kitchen as if I would see Marisol pop up at any moment. She'd be the only reason why I would stay here. What about my daughter? What if I wasn't here? Would she be able to fend off the boy? "I'd love to help you with that project, I really would, but I don't want to take advantage of our friendship. And I know this sounds crazy, but I need to be here."

"I'll bunk out at your house, then. Just for tonight. I mean, surely you know I'm not trying to be pushy. I'm really concerned. If that boy tried to drown you, who's to say he won't attack you again? I don't want you to be by yourself there."

I leaned back and looked around the corner into my living room. No way was big, tall Jesse Clarke going to make a comfortable bed for himself on my wicker couch. But I did see an air mattress in the upstairs closet. To be honest, I liked the idea of someone else being here. I just couldn't leave Marisol. What if she didn't follow me?

"That sounds great. Would you mind? And bring whatever information you have about the McIntyre family. Maybe if we dig a little deeper, we could find something to help us identify this boy. The thought of those two working together is more horrifying."

The phone line began to whine, and there was a strange crunching sound like the connection was breaking up.

"Jesse? Jesse, can you hear me?" And then the phone went dead. *Okay, that's just weird.* I had to call the phone company about this. Twice in one week could not be a coincidence. I felt my phone vibrating in my pocket. It was a text from Jesse: *I'll be there in fifteen minutes.* I breathed a sigh of relief and texted him back a smiley face.

I made some sweet tea, cleared my kitchen table and plundered the refrigerator for something I could whip up for lunch. A light tapping on my back door drew me away from my search. No one ever used the back door, no one but Marisol and Loxley. *Marisol!* I hurried to open it but didn't see any little girls running away. There was no one there, nothing except a lone bluebonnet. I picked up the dark blue flower and held it. *Marisol. Thank you.* I went back into the house and found a small bottle to use as a vase. I filled it with water and put the flower on the kitchen table. We needed some good luck. I stared at the flower and experienced all sorts of emotions waiting for Jesse to arrive. True to his word, he showed up promptly with armloads of books, an overnight bag and a plastic crate of folders.

"Goodness. You came prepared. Let me help you." I grabbed the plastic file folder bin, surprised at the weight. "You weren't kidding when you said you had a heck of a lot of research." He shook his head, and I admired the glasses he was wearing today. "Hey, those look good on you." He gave me a half grin, and we walked into the kitchen and deposited all of the materials on the table. "Would you like a glass of tea?"

"Sure. Sounds great. Did you hear anything from Hannah yet? I guess you know Ree-Ree is all over this. She's gonna come over sometime today. She happened to be at the house when you called and overheard everything."

"It's no bother. I like your cousin. I just hope it's not unsafe to have people around. I mean, my God. I would never have imagined anything like that happening to me. It was like something out of a movie. A horror movie." I shivered at the memory of the boy grabbing my ankle and pulling me down into the river. If I wasn't such a good swimmer, if I wasn't determined to live, I wouldn't be standing here right now. *No, I'd be with Marisol. Is that such a bad thing?* I walked over to the refrigerator and poured Jesse a glass of tea. I set it down in front of him and watched him arrange stacks of papers on the table. "Where do we start? Tell me what you know about the McIntyre family, in a nutshell."

"Mariana McIntyre, the young woman who was murdered, her father's name was Robert 'Bull' McIntyre. And just like his name suggests, he was a force of nature all by himself. It was strange that anyone would want to build a mansion out here in the middle of nowhere, but he was determined to do it. Rumor has it that there used to be another house on this property before Summerleigh, but it burned to the ground. The records from that time—probably in the early 1830s—are not reliable, and there isn't much information about who owned this property then. So as far as official records go, we can only go back to the McIntyre family. Mariana had just turned sixteen when she was found dead. Let me see if I can find a copy of the actual newspaper clipping. I have it here somewhere." Jesse shuffled through his records until he found what he was looking for. "Ah, here it is."

He slid it to me, and I silently read the headline: McIntyre Mystery Murder Friday Night. I read and reread the tiny article, but there wasn't much information there except for Mariana's age and a mention of her brother and father.

"Is that it? Did they ever find her killer?"

"I haven't found any record of anyone being charged with her murder. I found nothing in any of the papers. To make matters worse, Summerleigh was full that night. It was her birthday celebration."

"God, she died on her birthday?"

"Yeah," he said. "After that article, I don't find even a mention of Mariana again. But Bull McIntyre went downhill fast. His lumber mill burned, and he was accused of all types of crimes, arson, murder—two men died in that mill fire. He refused to help their families afterward. He accused them of arson and even threatened lawsuits against their widows. The women gave up their claims, but the damage had been done. All of George County turned against him. People had nothing to do with him after that, and everyone pointed at him anytime something went wrong in Desire."

"Do you think he did it? Could it have been him I saw at the river?"

"I don't know, but we shouldn't rule out Mariana's brothers. She had two, a younger one and an older one. The younger one's name has been lost, but I do know both boys' names started with the letter J. Military records indicate that a Jameson McIntyre enlisted in the Mississippi militia around the time of Mariana's death, but he was never seen or heard from again. But you have to remember that times were different then. If people wanted to get lost, they could."

"So he disappeared after her murder?"

"I can't be sure. It's pretty close, as far as timelines go."

"This other McIntyre, the younger boy, I wonder what his name is. Hannah told me that she believed I had some authority with the ghost because I own the house now. She thinks if I knew his name, I could command him to leave. Any chance we'll find it in here?"

"I've looked for years," he confessed as he opened a folder. Seeing my expression, he quickly added, "But today might be my lucky day."

I accepted the folder and skimmed through the lists of births and deaths. Geesh, Jesse had put in a lot of time on this. After a few minutes of paper shuffling, I sat back and closed my eyes. This wasn't the time to get a headache, but I could feel one coming on. The house was quiet except for the ice cracking in Jesse's glass. I half expected to hear that light tapping again at the back door. For a moment, I wondered what it would be like for Jesse to meet Marisol. Would she like him? Surely she would have. He was kind and loving, just like Eddie used to be before the drugs sucked his soul dry. And then my house phone rang. I gasped and put my hand on my chest. "Excuse me. That must be Hannah." I picked up and said, "Hello?"

"Jerica, this is Ben, Ben Hartley. I'm on my way to Summerleigh. I have something to tell you. Please, promise me you'll wait for me to arrive."

"Wait for what, Ben? Are you okay?" I looked at Jesse, who raised his eyebrows.

"It's something I should have told you a long time ago. I'm driving down. Be there in about an hour." And with that, he clicked the phone down and the line went dead.

"Ben?" I held the phone up and put it back on the base. I turned to Jesse and said, "You're never gonna believe this, but Ben Hartley is on the way here. He says there's something he has to tell me."

"Well, I guess we might as well keep plowing through. There is a chance I missed something. I mean, this is a lot of information. You ready to dig deep?"

My stomach was growling, but my fear was growing too. I chewed on my bottom lip, wondering what in the world Ben wanted to tell me. And why couldn't he have told me on the phone? Or the other day? There was nothing to do but wait. I took my seat beside Jesse and began shuffling through the papers, looking for any reference to the McIntyre family that I could find. This might be the slowest hour of my life.

I suddenly snapped my fingers. "Wait a second. That book. I found a book in the potting shed, and I've been meaning to show it to you. I think I put it in the bookcase."

"What book?" Jesse looked up from a land owner's record he was flipping through.

"I found it a few months ago and forgot all about it. It was the day I heard the girls giggling outside the potting shed." I rifled through the bookcase in the living room and found the dusty old book in a drawer. "Here it is. The writing is faint, but I think the name inside is McIntyre."

I leaned over him as he examined the cover. There was no title, and the cover appeared a bit worse for wear. It wasn't a large book, more like a journal. He flipped it open and laid it on the table in front of him. "Hey, turn that light on. You're right, this ink is pretty faded."

"I think it's some sort of record. Maybe for plants? Was Mr. McIntyre a botanist?"

"Not that I know of. I wish I understood all these notations. Look, there are several columns, but the headings are too faded to read. Maybe these are flower species? I need a magnifying glass to make this out."

"I don't have one." I peered closer. "The more I look at it, I don't think those are flower names. Aren't those usually Latin? That one there," I said as I pointed at the page, "that's C-L-A-U-D-E-T-T-E something or other. And that one there, A-R-, is that an I? Or an L? It could be A-R-I-C-E-L-I. Grab a pen, Jesse. Hey, I'll use my phone to magnify the writing."

"Brilliant," he said as he slid the book to me and reached for a notebook.

Surprisingly, the hour didn't drag by. By the end of it, we were looking at a list of names, places and strange descriptions. At the very back of the book, we found the faint signature of Jameson P. McIntyre.

At least we'd solved one mystery and confirmed the name of one of the McIntyre sons. Little did we know that things were about to get even stranger.

## *Chapter Ten—Jerica*

Jesse and I were still waiting for Ben to arrive. So far, he was a no-show. The afternoon was burning away; we were losing daylight, and I began to feel anxious. Not just at the idea of going into the house at night but because Ben had seemed so frail when last I saw him. I couldn't understand his change of heart. He'd done everything he could to make sure I came to Summerleigh, leaving me those keys and walking out of the Sunrise Retirement Home without another word. If he hadn't shown up, I would never have fallen in love with the place and the long-lost Belle family. Now he wanted to send me back to Virginia?

Yeah, color me confused. I checked the clock again. It was after four now. If he was coming from Jackson, he should've been here an hour ago. I turned to Jesse, unable to hide the worry I felt.

"Does Ben have any relatives in the area that you know about? Someone we could contact?"

"No. I can't think of anyone. But you know how Ben is, Jerica. He'll be here soon, and if he's not, we can contact the state troopers or somebody."

Someone tapped on the front door, and I hoped and prayed that it was Ben Hartley. Instead, it was Hannah. I'd been so worried about Ben that I completely forgot about her. She was here with two people I didn't know, so I gathered she'd gotten my voicemail that I wanted to move forward with our investigation into Summerleigh.

"Hey, Hannah. Please come in. I'm so glad you could make it."

Hannah clutched her purse as she always did and smiled nervously before introducing me to her friends. "Thanks for inviting me. These are two of my colleagues, Amy Whitehead and Rex Nylund. Both have a lot of experience in the paranormal field. Amy's here to help me with the technical aspects of our investigation, and Rex has other skills. He's a sensitive." Amy nodded, and Rex extended his hand. I shook it politely and invited them into the kitchen where Jesse was tidying up our research to make room for them.

"Hey, Hannah," he said, glancing over his shoulder. "Hey, y'all," he said politely to Rex and Amy as he arranged his papers in the plastic bin and slid it out of the way.

"Jesse, I didn't know you were here," Hannah said, giving him a sunny smile. That was a rare thing—she was friendly but not one to smile much. I invited everyone to have a seat around the table. Since we were one chair short, I pulled the extra one up from its usual spot near the Princess telephone.

Rex said, "I hear you have a negative entity at Summerleigh. I can't say I'm surprised, considering all of the history that's happened on this property. What is it you hope we can do for you, Jerica?"

"I'm hoping to get rid of him. I mean, if he were the peaceful sort of spirit, I wouldn't mind him being there. But slamming doors and scaring people? I can't have that happening all the time."

"Hannah told us that the activity ramped up when you guys began to renovate. That's not uncommon. Any particular hot spots?" Amy asked in a soft voice as she whipped out a notebook and pencil.

"Yes, that is correct. The house was empty for quite some time before I got here. I was hoping to change all that. I think most of the activity happens on the second floor, in the nursery and the attic."

Rex leaned forward and rested his chin on his folded hands. "I want you to understand that I am a sensitive, but I'm not an exorcist, so I don't have any special skills for ousting ghosts. But I will be glad to lend whatever skills I do have to help you navigate this situation. I understand it can be frightening to have that activity happening around you."

Jesse nodded in agreement. "The doors on the top floor slammed so hard I thought the place was going to fall in. It was the scariest darn thing I've ever seen. If I hadn't seen it myself, I'm not sure I would believe it. We've been working in that house for weeks and have not had any problems. But now, it's straight-up dangerous. Jerica, tell them what happened to you today at the river."

All eyes were on me, and I fought the urge to kick Jesse under the table. Since he brought it up, I told the group what happened earlier and then concluded, "And Mr. Daughdrill was standing on the bank watching. Like he wanted me to drown, like he expected me to die. I guess I can understand why he would want to come after me. At least Harper went to her grave not knowing what a monster he really was, but I know him for who he is. He was never the kind of man who liked it when a woman had the upper hand on him. I know the type." I avoided looking in Jesse's direction. I hadn't meant to drop hints about my past like that.

"That's not quite true. She knew. Harper knew," a voice from behind me whispered. I spun around to see Ben Hartley standing in my kitchen drenched with sweat.

"Ben! I didn't hear you come in. Please have a seat. Would you like something to drink?" Ben's face looked pale, and his lips were colorless.

"Yes. Water, please."

"What happened to you, Ben?"

"I had a flat, and I'm not as spry as I used to be."

I handed him a glass of water and said, "These are my friends, Ben. This is Hannah, and this is Amy and Rex. They're here to help me with the house."

With shaking hands, Ben sipped the water. "I don't think you understand, Jerica. Some of those spirits can't be pacified, and no amount of pleading with them is going to change that. They are dead and gone, and there's nothing more you can do for them."

The kitchen was so quiet you could hear a pin drop. I didn't want him to get worked up again, not after what he'd been through already. In an attempt to steer the conversation in another direction I asked, "What do you mean, Ben? What did Harper know? Did Mr. Daughdrill die that night?"

Ben put his empty glass on the table and buried his face in his hands. He sobbed, and I put my arm around him. What was it about this man that made me want to protect him? He seemed so broken, but I had no idea why. Hannah, Rex and Amy excused themselves and hurried off to the living room to give us some privacy.

Jesse grabbed some tissues and handed them to him. Ben said, "I'm so sorry, Jerica. I don't mean to blubber like a child. And I know it was a long time ago, but it doesn't make it any easier. You understand."

I nodded. "Tell us what happened. What did Harper know?"

"Daughdrill didn't die that night. She told me about it later, after we had become better friends. She and Addison were like my own two sisters. I admit I had a bit of a crush on Harper back then. Maybe I still do. Old man Daughdrill hated me. He'd complain to Mrs. Belle when I came around, but she didn't say a word to Harper. I think she was proud of her, thankful in her own twisted way, but she would never say so. Oh no. She was never the kind of woman to admit she needed anyone. But really, she was needier than everyone."

"Go on, Ben. Tell me more about Harper."

"Mr. Daughdrill started coming around the school to see Addison. He would bring her presents like jewelry, but she never left with him. Harper was always there, running defense. But he was a master at manipulation, and he succeeded in driving a wedge between them, at least for a little while. Before he died, he practically moved into the house and took over. Her mother didn't say a word." Ben began to tear up again. "Harper wouldn't want you to be in danger, Jerica. Please promise me you'll stop the renovation. Let sleeping dogs lie, Jerica. Go back home and have a happy life."

Jesse couldn't hide his surprise. "Why, Ben? You haven't given her a reason except to say bad things happened to the Belle girls. We know that. Don't you think it's time to let some sunshine into the place? Let Summerleigh breathe again?"

"You can't see it. You see the house and want to love it, but nobody is happy there. Nobody is ever happy at Summerleigh. John Belle thought he could fix the place up. Look where it got him. Jeopardy, Addison, Harper...they're all gone. You don't understand. You haven't seen what I've seen." He sobbed again.

I cast an eye at Jesse and nodded my head toward the living room. Thankfully, he got the message and immediately left to apologize to Hannah and her friends. I heard the front door open and close as they left. I'd have to call her later.

More than anything, I wanted to know who that little boy was, but it wouldn't be today. Ben Hartley was in no shape to drive home, and I couldn't in good conscience ignore his wishes. Not while he was here, anyway. I sat quietly and waited for him to regain his composure. Jesse returned and sat at the table with us. I was glad to have him there.

"Now tell us everything, Ben. What have you seen at Summerleigh that makes you so afraid?"

"I've seen the devil there, Jerica. And he's not going to leave. It was his place before they ever built Summerleigh. This is old land. Lots of deadly things happened here. Even the local native tribes avoided this patch of land. I tried to warn Harper. I told her what I knew, what my grandfather told me, but she didn't listen. Not until it was too late." Ben sounded confused, and it set off alarms in my nurse's brain. *I know these symptoms, don't I?* "At least she made it out alive. I am glad for that. I loved Harper Belle, you know. It broke my heart when she married that Hayes fella, but it is what it is. Water under the bridge." He wiped at his eyes again. "When I lived here, I woke up to find flowers on my doorstep every now and then. How about you?"

I glanced at the flower on the table. It had withered a bit but was still a vibrant shade of blue. My heart sank. I wanted to believe Marisol had brought me those flowers. Had I been wrong?

"Yes, I've found flowers a few times."

"Ah, but you never know who's bringing them. Be careful what you invite into your home, Jerica Poole. Be really careful. Some things aren't that easy to get rid of."

Jesse stared hard at the old man, and I could see the uncertainty on his face. Ignoring the icy-cold feeling I had, I glanced at the clock. Suppertime. That's what Ben needed, food and some rest.

"Jesse, how do you feel about grilling some pork chops? I've got some in the refrigerator. Are you hungry, Ben?"

"Yes, but I thought you wanted to hear everything."

"I do, but right now I want to eat. Why don't you get freshened up while Jesse and I whip up some grub?"

"That would be lovely. Thank you. I'll do that." He wandered off to the bathroom. Of course, he didn't have to ask where it was. He'd lived here. He knew this house inside and out. And he knew Summerleigh.

Jesse touched my arm. "I hope you don't intend to let him stay here. Something seems off about him. I know you want to see him as a sweet old man and everything, but I can't shake the feeling that something is wrong."

"I agree. But the less he hears about the house, the better off he'll be. I don't think Ben is well. I really don't. Let's cook supper and go from there. Thank you for being so patient with him. And me."

Jesse grinned down at me and said, "Just show me the way to the grill."

"Just out back on the patio." I kissed his cheek playfully. He paused, like he wanted more, but Ben came back into the kitchen.

"I'm not interrupting you all, am I?"

"Not at all, Ben. Have a seat while I prep these chops."

And for the next few hours, nobody talked about Summerleigh or ghosts. It was nice to pretend that everything was okay. Unfortunately, it was just the calm before the storm.

## *Chapter Eleven—Harper*

"Loxley wasn't at school today, Momma. Can't we go see her?"

A haze of cigarette smoke swirled around my mother's face, and she wore her usual lost expression. She always looked like this when she'd spent the previous night drinking, and she did that more and more as of late. "She's better off with Dot. In fact, you'd all be better off." And she was still drunk.

I hung up the phone and stared at the back of her head. Her hair was unbrushed and unwashed. She wasn't dressed either. Addison and I would have to hoof it, and quickly, if we were going to make it to school on time. One more tardy and I would face Mr. Alfred's wrath. And possibly his paddle. Too bad he couldn't paddle Momma.

"Where's Jeopardy this morning? Jeopardy?" It of course wasn't Jep but Addison. She came into the kitchen wearing new shoes, and her hair was brushed and tidy.

"Morning, Momma. What's for breakfast, Harper?" she said as she frowned at the empty table.

*Am I the only sane one around here?*

"You don't have time for breakfast, your majesty. We're walking to school this morning," I said as I picked up my books from the table and slung my purse over my shoulder.

"I can't walk to school in these shoes. They're brand new!" she whined as she pursed her pouty lips. "Grandfather would be so mad if I scuffed them up before he saw me in them."

That woke Momma up from her stupor. She rose to her wobbly feet and put her hands on the table to steady herself. "What did you say? Who's buying you shoes, Addison Lee?"

Addison backed away from Momma, and I pushed her behind me as I reached for the back door. "We better go, Addison."

"Okay," she said as she scurried out of Summerleigh. "Bye, Momma." I could hear her voice breaking up as she sailed down the back steps.

"Addison, you get back here!" Momma shouted after her.

I closed the door and left Momma to stew in her own juices. I caught up with Addison around the corner of the house. The overgrown hydrangeas made the perfect hiding spot. "Come on out, Addie. She's too drunk to follow us to school. Take your shoes off if you're worried about getting them dirty, but the walk might be hard on your feet."

Addison clutched her notebook to her chest and looked down at her shoes. "These are the nicest shoes I've ever owned." She didn't take them off, and we walked together down Hurlette.

I smiled at her. "Yes, they're very nice."

Addison smiled back, but her expression changed. Daddy always said she would make a horrible poker player. She could never hide her emotions. "I'm sorry, Harper." She grabbed my arm gently. "I tried to get you a pair too, but you know how Grandfather is. Maybe if you apologized to him, he'd like you again. I tried to explain it to him, how hard it was to live with Momma, but I think...I think you really hurt him. I mean, you did beat him with that poker."

I couldn't believe my ears. It was too early in the day to be stupefied twice. "He was beating Momma, Addison. How can you take his side? You're my sister."

"I know, and I love you, Harper, but you can be so strong-willed sometimes."

"Where did you hear that?" I asked suspiciously. I needn't have wondered. Mr. Daughdrill pulled up in his long black Master DeLuxe and rolled his window down.

"Would you like a ride to school, Addison? I'm going to town. I'll be happy to take you so you don't get caught in the rain."

"Sure," she said, but then she looked at me. "But can Harper go too? Like you said, it might rain and all."

He cast a steely look at me. Now, Mr. Daughdrill would have made a fine poker player. You never knew what he was thinking. Never. "Of course, dear. Hop in, girls. You wouldn't want to be late. That's not the Daughdrill way. Your mother was never late for school. Not one day."

"We're not Daughdrills. We're Belles," I murmured as I walked to the car. Addison shot me an ugly grimace, and I rolled my eyes. I climbed in the back seat and listened to the radio as we pulled up into the schoolyard. I immediately began searching for Aunt Dot's convertible but didn't see it. I wondered if Loxley would be in school today, but I didn't dare ask Mr. Daughdrill. When we arrived at school, I got out of the car and gave a half-hearted thank-you.

"Harper, a word of advice." He waved me toward him, but I didn't step any closer. "Don't ruin things for Addison. She has a real future; she's such a lovely young lady. It's not attractive for a girl to be jealous of her sister."

"I'm not jealous of my sister. And I have three of them, remember?" Cars were pulling in behind his, and I took another step back.

"Stay out of trouble, Harper. We can't afford another scandal. I'll see you girls after school. Make sure you are here and ready to go home."

I stared after him as he pulled off. Addison was already in the schoolhouse; she'd left me behind, probably anxious to show off her new shoes. I guess I really couldn't blame her. We rarely had new things. But at what cost? Why would he do that? I couldn't imagine Mr. Daughdrill doing anything that didn't benefit him directly.

The day dragged by. The only bright spot was a surprise invitation to go fishing with Benny and his little cousin Angie. I agreed to meet them at the river at four o'clock but had second thoughts later. I hadn't been to the river since Jeopardy disappeared. Why was it nobody said her name anymore? I had that deputy's phone number somewhere, and I made up my mind then and there to call him. Momma wasn't going to do it, and I wanted my sister to come home.

I waited outside the school after the bell, but Mr. Daughdrill didn't show up, and neither did my sister. It would be very much like him to leave me behind as a way to teach me a lesson. Yes, very much like him.

"Hey, Arnette?" I caught my friend as she walked out with her steady, a tall, skinny kid named Roger. "Have you seen Addison?"

"She left a few minutes ago. With your grandfather, I think. Did you see them, Roger? I ducked inside to get my sweater."

Roger squinched his eyes and said, "You know, I think she did leave in that big black car. The new one."

"Was she alone?" I asked.

He shook his head. "No, her friend Bobbie Ann was with her. Need a ride? Did they leave you behind, Harper?"

"Yes, please. I guess she forgot all about me."

Arnette rolled her eyes. "Sisters. I'm glad I have Roger here. Let's take Harper home. It's on the way to my house."

"Sure thing, sweetie."

Arnette shook her head. I could tell she didn't like his nickname for her, but at least he was a nice guy. The ride home was long, not because the company was bad but because I was worried about my sisters. Loxley was with Aunt Dot, absent again today. Addison was off with our grandfather, and Momma was probably drinking herself to death. And God only knew where Jeopardy was. I didn't want to believe she was really a ghost. That would mean she was dead, right?

We pulled into the driveway, and I got out of the truck before it stopped. "Thanks, you two. I'll buy you both a Coke sometime."

"Sounds great. Bye, Harper," Arnette said with a smile.

"Bye," I said as I walked up the steps of Summerleigh. I rarely came in the front door, but it was unlocked and I walked right inside.

I walked through the Great Room into the parlor. My grandfather was lounging in the red velvet chair, the radio on low, the newspaper in his lap. He sucked on his pipe and smiled at me. I didn't return the smile. "Where's Addison?"

As if she'd heard me, Addie walked into the room from the bedroom hallway. "Hey, Harper. Just the person I'm looking for. What do you think? Pink sweater with the green dress or the blue one? I'm not sure. Grandfather says pink, but I kind of like the blue." She strutted around in her new dress and spun around for our grandfather, who complimented her on the color...and the fit.

"I don't know," I grumbled at her as I headed into the kitchen to find something to eat. Momma was on the phone, obviously with Aunt Dot, and I tried not to eavesdrop. When I opened the refrigerator, I almost passed out. It was loaded with food, a nice chunk of cheese, milk, butter and fruit galore. I couldn't help but notice that these were all Addison's favorites.

"You bring her home, Dot, or I'm going to call the police." She paused and then said, "No, he's not. I haven't seen him. Now bring me my daughter." She slammed the phone down and stubbed out her skinny cigarette in her seashell-shaped ashtray. "There you are. I've got some chicken laid out for supper. Are you up to frying it? I need to go lie down. I can feel a headache coming on."

"No. I already have plans."

"Well, those plans will have to wait. Someone needs to cook supper, Harper." She walked out of the kitchen with her hand on her forehead.

I sighed, but nobody heard me. *Same old, same old.* Just then, I heard Ben calling me from the screen door. "Hey, we've been waiting for you at the river. You ready to go?"

I reached for a few strawberries and put the pint back in the refrigerator. I wasn't cooking supper. I wasn't doing any of it. I was going fishing. "You got a pole for me?"

"Yep, and it's ready to go." Ben smiled and showed his missing tooth. I liked him more by the minute. "All right. Let's go."

We only caught two small fish, but it wasn't a total loss. Ben was quiet and his little cousin even quieter. It was a nice evening tossing lines in the water. We talked a little, more than I thought we would. I didn't come back until after dark, and I was bone-tired. I had homework, but somehow, it didn't seem that important anymore. They must have managed supper because although the kitchen was tidy when I came in the back door, I could smell the remnants of fried chicken. I opened the refrigerator hoping to find a piece, but there wasn't any left. Mr. Daugh-drill must have stayed for dinner. I grabbed some more strawberries and headed to my room. But then I heard the pop of Momma's lighter and saw her face illuminated in the yellow light.

"Awful late, Harper Louise. I guess you were out with a boy."

"It's not that late. Only nine o'clock. I lost track of time is all."

"It's easy to do when you're in someone's arms," she said as she spat a stray bit of tobacco leaf out of her mouth and eyed me. She had her arm crooked over the back of her chair. I couldn't smell any alcohol, but I had to be careful. Any minute, Momma could turn on you. I glanced around carefully and spotted a skillet on the stove. She followed my eyes and tilted her head up.

"I wasn't in anyone's arms. I'm only fifteen, Momma. I went fishing is all."

She took a deep drag off her skinny cigarette and said in a quiet voice, "You'll have to sleep upstairs tonight. Mr. Daughdrill is sleeping in your room. I expect he will sleep in there for a few nights at least."

"What? Why is he here?"

She didn't answer my question. "I left you some blankets on the couch. I guess you could sleep on it if you don't mind the smell. It really needs to be cleaned, Harper."

"Why is he in my bed? Don't you remember how he treated you?"

"That's all over now, and I've forgiven him. And you should too, dear. It's what's best for us all. Now, don't make a fuss. Go to sleep. You have school in the morning, in case you forgot. I swear, you behave more like your sister every day."

I stomped my foot. "Good! I want to be like her. And why can't you say her name, Momma? Do you remember her name? Jeopardy! Why can't you say her name?" I was shouting now, but there was nothing I could do about it.

"Of course I do. You think I could forget her? You think I don't see her all the time? I wish...I wish a lot of things, but wishing don't make it reality. Go to bed, Harper."

"I'm not sleeping on the couch."

"You can't sleep with Addison. She's ill and can't be disturbed."

"So you want me to go upstairs and sleep with the ghosts, then?" I wasn't joking. The idea of sleeping in Jeopardy's castle room or any other room on that floor frightened me. Jep had always been braver than me.

"You know perfectly well your sister would never hurt you. Go to bed."

And in that moment, I knew Momma believed Jeopardy was dead. But why did she think that? I lay on the couch first, but it was so uncomfortable that I couldn't sleep. I could smell Mr. Daughdrill's pipe tobacco too, and the odor made me squeamish. I tiptoed to Addison's room. I could hear Mr. Daughdrill snoring in my room before I even got into the hallway. Addie was out like a light. I crept back down the hall and retrieved my blanket and pillow.

I felt like I was going into exile, like I was now officially banned from the family. I didn't fit in anymore. I wasn't wanted.

Was this how Jeopardy felt?

*I haven't given up on you, Jep. I love you. You are the best sister a girl ever had. I'll bring you home. I swear, as God is my witness, I swear.* With fat tears, I made the trek up the stairs and walked down the dark hallway to the attic. I heard nothing, I saw nothing, and I kept my eyes ahead of me.

It was as if the ghosts were expecting me and welcomed me. I was one of them now. Or I would be soon.

The attic door opened with a creak. I closed it behind me and stood in the dark trying to adjust my eyes to the dimness. Jeopardy's pallet was under the window. I tossed my blanket on top of hers and put my pillow beside hers. Absolutely exhausted, I curled up in a ball and clutched her pillow, which still held her sweet, wild scent. She smelled like sunshine and wildflowers and tobacco. She smelled like life...but not anymore.

*Where are you, Jeopardy Belle? Why did you leave me?*

I cried myself to sleep and woke up early as the sun was beginning to rise. My body was stiff and achy all over from sleeping on the floor. I missed my comfortable bed, but I doubted that I would ever sleep in it again. I could hear the signs of life in the house even before I opened my eyes.

*Mariana, oh Mariana. Open your eyes. Open them. Open your eyes. Look what I have...*

"What? Ben?" I heard a boy's voice, but I couldn't fathom who it could be. There were no boys in this house, especially not up here. I blinked against the sunlight that streamed through the window. I saw him for only the briefest of seconds.

It was a boy with large dark eyes, black hair and pale skin. He held a pair of scissors in one hand and a lock of my hair in the other. I screamed as he vanished, and my hand immediately went to my hair.

I couldn't believe it, but the ghost had cut a lock of my hair. It was gone. I looked around the bed and saw nothing. Had I cut my hair in my sleep? No, of course not. I didn't even own a pair of scissors.

I scooted away from the pallet and put my back against the wall, waiting for my heart to stop racing. There were indeed ghosts here. And one of them had a pair of scissors. Loxley had been telling the truth all along.

I ran as fast as I could out of the attic and down the stairs. I didn't stop until I found Addison. Instantly, she put her arms around me. "It's okay, Harper. You can sleep with me tonight. You can stay with me. You don't ever have to go upstairs again."

I would hold her to that promise.

# Chapter Twelve—Jerica

I glanced at the clock, surprised to see that it was eight o'clock already. I could hear men's voices downstairs. *Must be Jesse and Ben.* I didn't wait for Marisol's hug. I'd given up on those. Instead, I clutched her purple bear to my chest and kissed it before climbing out of bed. It wasn't her favorite toy, but it was the only one I had left. Eddie had taken everything else. I suddenly felt the urge to call the detective handling his case to get more details on how things had turned out, but I resisted. Yeah, I wanted Eddie to rot under the jail, but as long as he was nowhere near me, I wasn't going to bother wasting any more time on him.

I found a white t-shirt and a pair of blue shorts to wear. It was going to be another hot day, and I had to get into that house somehow without upsetting Ben too much. I wondered how Jesse had fared on the wicker sofa. I heard a vehicle pull out of the driveway. Was that Jesse? Ben? I'd find out in a minute, but first I had to brush this hair of mine. I began brushing the knots out and was surprised to find a chunk of it was missing.

A sizable chunk.

Oh my God! Was I going bald? I searched my bed for the missing hair, but there was nothing there. I didn't know why I couldn't remember what happened to it. I hadn't had a drop to drink last night and couldn't remember the last time I'd taken a pill, since I'd never found a new doctor to get those new prescriptions. But whether I remembered it or not, a good half-inch of my hair had been cut, and whoever had done the deed had chunked it up big time. No, wait. He'd cut several chunks of my hair. And now I had a fragmentary memory of the sound of heavy scissors.

"What in the..." Well, there were only two other people in my house. But would either Jesse or Ben pull such a prank? Was this some sort of south Mississippi joke?

"You guys, is this a joke?" I said as I walked into the kitchen, holding up my hair to show them the cut spot. The room was empty except for a note on the table written in Jesse's neat handwriting.

*Taking Ben to town to buy a new tire. His spare won't make it home. I called Hannah. They'll be back over after Ben leaves. Made you some coffee and cinnamon rolls.*

*-J*

He didn't say, "Hey, I took some hair," so I must be losing my mind. I poured a cup of coffee and marched back upstairs to try and do something with my mop. The struggle was real. I finally pulled on a ball cap and pulled my ponytail out the back. This would have to do until I could see a stylist about my unwanted haircut.

*That boy, the ghost that scared Harper in my dream, didn't he have a pair of scissors?* The creepy crawlies covered my body, but the sensation did not fill me with fear as it might have before. No, I was feeling something else now. I was feeling pissed off.

First, he tries to drown me in the river, and now he cuts my hair off? What was wrong with this ghost? Did he think I was Mariana? Maybe he thought he screwed up the first time and wanted to come back to finish the job now?

I waited around for a few minutes and decided to take a walk to Summerleigh. I wanted some answers, and I wanted them yesterday. And by heavens, I was going to get them. I didn't know what I expected to learn, but I finished my coffee and walked out of the caretaker's cottage, leaving the door unlocked in case Jesse beat me home. I walked down the gravel pathway and went to the back door of Summerleigh. I knocked politely, as I nearly always did when I came in through this entrance. Nobody answered, of course, but for a moment I imagined I heard a chair slide under the table. *Am I interrupting breakfast, Harper?*

"It's me, Jerica Poole," I announced as I opened the door. I dreaded hearing the sounds of doors closing again in this breezy old house, so I propped a chair against the door to keep it open. "I'm not here to bother anyone, Harper. I'm still your friend."

*Jerica...*

Someone whispered my name. But who?

"Yes, it's me. I'm here by myself, Harper. Addison, Jeopardy. I'm here by myself. I'm going to walk through Summerleigh. I don't want to disturb you, but I need to find the boy. He cut my hair last night, and I want to know why."

And then I heard nothing but a breeze blowing in over the sink. Hey, wasn't that window closed? It had to be. I walked over to the window, and sure enough, it was closed. So where was that breeze coming from? We hadn't installed the new air conditioning system yet. I raised my hand above my head. No, this wasn't a draft. It was coming from the window. I could feel it up there too. What was that? There was a small stepladder in the kitchen, which I moved under the window so I could take down the curtains. Maybe the window wasn't sealed properly. Maybe air was getting in through a loose shim that we'd neglected to caulk. Anything was possible.

I stood on the ladder and reached above the window. Aha! That was it. It was breezy out, and this crack in the window seal was making the curtains flutter. I felt like a true paranormal investigator on one of the shows that Eddie used to enjoy watching. "Debunked," I announced proudly as I started to climb back down the short ladder.

But then I saw a face looking back at me from the other side of the window. It was the angriest face I'd ever seen. With red eyes in a shriveled skull, it bared its yellowed teeth at me. I knew who I was looking at. This was the very dead Mr. Daughdrill. With a scream of surprise, I fell backward and hit my head so hard that I saw stars.

And then I felt warm blood trickling down my neck. "Harper..." I whispered as everything faded.

Then I heard nothing at all.

# Chapter Thirteen—Jerica

"Come on, Jeopardy. You'll make us late again." I heard a woman's voice behind me and recognized it as belonging to Jeopardy's Aunt Dot. I clutched her hand. Dot was so pretty, far prettier than her sister. Why couldn't anyone else see it, especially Dot?

"Please, I'm not Jeopardy. My name is Jerica, Jerica Poole."

"Jeopardy Belle, what did your Daddy tell you about lying?" Aunt Dot led me to the mirror in her room and pointed at me. The face looking back wasn't mine. I wasn't Jerica Poole anymore. I was truly Jeopardy Belle. Or at least I was her in this dream or whatever it was.

"John Belle, come see your daughter. She's playing that game again, you know, the one where she pretends she's somebody else."

John walked into the bathroom and leaned against the doorframe in his white overalls and a white t-shirt. He was as handsome today as he was the day I met him on the front porch of the caretaker's cottage.

"Please tell her, JB. You know who I am. You must know I'm not your daughter. I'm Jerica Poole." A gleam of recognition was in his eyes, but he couldn't answer me because Aunt Dot stepped in the way and closed the door between us.

"Jeopardy Belle, stop playing these games and get ready. We aren't going to have enough time to get you up to that school before Harper's big debut, and it's so important to her that you go."

*No, this is all wrong. John Jeffrey Belle had already died when Harper went to the Harvest Dance.* "Let me out of here. I have to go. I have to go now. I don't belong here." And then I saw that Aunt Dot had a pair of silver scissors in her hand.

"Dot? What are you doing with those?"

Aunt Dot's eyes were no longer a pretty soft blue, and her face had lost its feminine softness. Her eyes were dark, like two bottomless pits with no white at all. The woman—or whatever it was—was not Jeopardy's Aunt Dot.

She shouted, "Give me what I want! I must have it!"

With a scream, I pushed her away as I closed my eyes and waited for the blow. I had nowhere to run, nowhere to go. I was trapped in the bathroom with this blade-wielding entity. I threw my hands up instinctively to fend off the attack.

It didn't come.

"Mommy, come with me."

I looked up to see Marisol in the doorway. The door was open, but the boy, the one who had pretended to be Aunt Dot, was in my way. "I command you to leave me alone! I own this house. It's not yours!" He wasn't as small as I remembered. No, not at all. This ghost was much older than the boy Jesse and I had seen on the second floor of Summerleigh.

And then he vanished, but I got the sense that he was not far away. I might have repelled him for the moment, but he was strong and persistent. And he wasn't going to give up until he got what he wanted, whatever that was. I shivered at the thought. I stepped into the hallway and looked left and right. Just as I turned to the right, I saw my daughter's shiny dark ringlets sailing behind her as she ran up the attic stairs.

"No, wait! Marisol, don't go in there. Please!"

She turned back to me for the briefest of seconds before she opened the door and walked inside. I had no choice but to follow her. I had waited so long to see her, and I wasn't going to pass up the opportunity now. I walked to the attic door, which stood open, put my foot on the step and waited to hear something. *What if this is another trick?* It didn't matter. I had to go!

"Marisol?" I cried softly. "If you're in here, please tell Mommy. I need to hear your voice, baby girl."

And then I heard her say as clear as a bell, "Where are you, Mommy? I'm waiting for you." As I stepped into the attic fully, I said a silent prayer. It was the same kind of prayer I had heard Harper pray so long ago. "Dear God, please don't let her be terrible. Please don't let my baby look like a monster. Please, God, help me."

There were many candles lit in the window near the place where Jeopardy's bed used to be. Jeopardy always liked candles. I knew that about her. Not many people knew it, but she enjoyed making candles. She'd spent many afternoons up here working with wax and wicks and molds, making her own creations. She had gotten quite good at it too, but like most things, once she mastered it, she got bored with it. But she loved this room; the ghosts never bothered her. And she loved her family, especially her sisters.

Yes, it was as if I could feel Jeopardy. I knew what she knew, what she felt. How strange that I would have this experience.

*Jeopardy. You have to know I tried to help you. Harper tried too.*

She didn't want to hear about that right now. She had something else on her mind, something she wanted to show me. She liked Marisol. Marisol reminded her of Loxley. And then I saw that my Marisol was sitting on the pallet with Jeopardy Belle. They were playing some sort of board game and having the time of their life. Marisol laughed as she tossed the dice and moved her blue piece around the board. I thought for a minute that they didn't see me, but I knew that wasn't true because I could feel and see and hear what Jeopardy felt and saw and heard. She knew I was there.

I didn't know what to do. Should I approach them? What if I walked toward them and then Marisol vanished? I couldn't live with that. Quietly, so I didn't disturb them, I sat on the floor a few feet away and stared at my baby's face. It was perfect and not broken at all. She was alive; her face was not pale, as it had been when I'd seen it last. It was sun-kissed, lovely and just as I remembered. My hands covered my mouth as I attempted to remain quiet. They wanted to show me something. Why didn't they just talk to me?

*Jeopardy? You know I'm here. Just tell me what it is you want me to know.*

She didn't answer. Instead, they began picking the pieces up and putting them back in the box. Was their game over already? I reached a shaking hand toward Marisol, but the air moved around me and I heard Jeopardy's raspy voice in my ear.

*No. It's forbidden.*

They wouldn't look at me or talk to me, except Jeopardy picked up a tiny book and let me see it before she put it in the Life board game box. They got up from the pallet and walked to the door with the game.

*Marisol, please, honey. Look at Mommy.*

She didn't, and I wanted to cry. I followed the girls as they left the castle room and went downstairs. To my surprise, they went not to the kitchen but instead to a small closet under the stairs. I don't think I'd noticed the hidden cabinet before, but now I wondered how I hadn't seen it. I was a carpenter's daughter, for pity's sake. Jeopardy put the game in the hidden door and closed it tight. She looked at me once more, then stood up and stretched out her hand to Marisol.

It was in that moment that my baby girl, my beautiful, perfect daughter, saw me. She didn't smile or frown. "Marisol..."

With a sad expression, she shook her head and spoke to me, but her mouth didn't move. "You can't come with me, Mommy. Not yet. Go back, okay? I'm okay, see? I'm with Jeopardy and Harper. Go back, Mommy."

I collapsed on the floor and cried my eyes out. After a few moments, I heard tiny footsteps approach me. My daughter put her arms around my neck, and I smelled her sweetness. I knew the feel of her skin, the smell of her hair. "My Marisol. I love you, Marisol. Mommy is so sorry."

And then she was gone. Those sweet arms around my neck vanished. It was a strange sensation to feel someone vanish beneath your fingers.

The next thing I knew, Jesse was there. The worried look on his handsome face caused me to worry. I smiled at him, in spite of the pain. "Marisol was here, Jesse. I saw her. She's here." And then I was out again.

When I woke up again, I was in a hospital room.

## *Chapter Fourteen—Jerica*

"Hey, Jerica. You finally decided to wake up?"

I glanced over to see Jesse in the chair beside my bed and gave him a wry smile. "I'm awake now. Don't these people know you aren't supposed to sleep if you have a concussion? What kind of hospital is this?"

"The closest. And for the record, you were told not to go to sleep. You snore, by the way."

"Good to know." I squinted at the light. "What happened? The details are a bit fuzzy." My mouth felt dry, and I had one hell of a headache.

Jesse pulled his chair close to my bed. "As near as I can tell, you fell off the ladder and smacked your head on the counter. But maybe there's something I'm missing."

And then it all came rushing back to me. The breeze, falling, seeing Jeopardy and Marisol. I swallowed and said, "I saw them, Jesse. I saw Jeopardy and Marisol. They were in the castle room." I saw my baby! Grief overwhelmed me again. It always seemed to creep up on me. I missed her every minute of every day, but sometimes the pain just heaped up and swept over me like an ocean tide. This was one of those moments. I couldn't help but cry. "Sorry to be such a mess."

"Hey, don't apologize."

I covered my eyes with my hands and forced myself to breathe. "I saw her, Jesse, as plain as day. She wasn't a ghost, not like the boy. She was beautiful and happy, but she wouldn't look at me. Not until the end. They were playing a game together, her and Jeopardy. A board game."

He squeezed my hand. We didn't get far into the conversation before the nurse stepped into the room. Without missing a beat, she said, "Great to see you awake. How do you feel? Any nausea? How is your vision?"

"I'm not sick at all, and I see perfectly. I'd like to go home now," I said as I tossed the covers off me.

"Whoa, Nellie. One step at a time, Mrs. Poole."

"It's Jerica."

"Okay, Jerica. Let's let the doctor check you out first. He'll be right over."

I slung my legs over the bed and steadied myself. I had to get back to Summerleigh. I had to find that game. It wasn't just a dream. It couldn't be. "You have five minutes," I answered as I waved goodbye to her. She didn't like my answer, but I didn't care. I had bigger fish to fry.

Jesse chuckled and stood ready to help me. "I have always heard that doctors make the worst patients, but I think nurses might give them a run for their money. What's the rush, Jerica?"

"How long have I been out?"

"About half a day. You hit your head pretty hard. I think they want to keep you for observation. I'm no medical professional and wouldn't know what to do if you had a seizure or something. Shouldn't you stay?"

"I'm not asking you to take care of me, Jesse Clarke. I just want my clothes."

He handed me a bag from the closet and said, "And I'm just concerned about you. I don't understand why you want to leave so badly."

"I have to go to Summerleigh, Jesse."

"Why?"

"Let me get dressed first, okay? I feel a little strange talking to you in my underwear."

He laughed at that. The tension of the moment dissipated, and he stepped out so I could put my clothes on. My head felt like it was on a swivel, but I was determined to leave. What if Marisol was still at Summerleigh? Seeing her only made me want to see her again. I wanted to hold her, comfort her. Whatever I could do to be with her. But I didn't say that to Jesse.

Thirty minutes later, we were headed back to what used to be Desire, Mississippi. Mobile was a pretty place with lots of fine homes, but it wasn't my home. Somewhere along the way, Summerleigh had become home. I loved every inch of the green grass, even the stubborn weeds and the wild woods that grew beside her. I loved the mud hole, the potting shed and every nook and cranny. It had been Harper and Jeopardy's home, and it was now mine. The doctor was polite and reminded me to take it easy and look out for the typical symptoms that can accompany a concussion. He suggested that I stay, but of course I did not. I couldn't. And quite honestly, I didn't understand the urgency, but I felt it deep in my bones.

I had to do what I was going to do now. It couldn't wait. Jeopardy Belle had been waiting too long.

When we arrived at Summerleigh, we sat in the truck a minute. I felt like Jesse had something he wanted to say to me, so I waited. Maybe he was waiting for me to say thank you? I probably should. I forgot about things like that sometimes. I didn't usually have anyone to thank except Anita. I missed my friend.

"Hey, thanks for checking up on me. If it weren't for you, I'd probably still be lying on the floor."

Jesse smiled good-naturedly. Gosh, he was such a nice guy. He kind of felt too good to be true. "You're welcome, Jerica. You can thank Ben, I suppose. He was adamant that I get back here. He's really afraid for you to be here. I don't understand it, but that's how he feels."

"Where has he gone?"

"He says he's going back home, but I don't know if I believe him. I think he needs medical help. He's almost obsessive about you and this place. It's concerning. Like I said, I don't know much about diseases, but it wouldn't surprise me if Ben wasn't getting good blood flow to his brain. For a few minutes, he was talking out of his head. Acting like you were Harper. He even called you that once or twice."

"It happens when you get old. Harper used to call me Jeopardy all the time."

"Still, be careful. I know you have a big heart and you want to help him, but...just use caution."

I leaned close to him. It was a bold move, but I was making it. "I promise to be careful. Now let me thank you properly." I pressed my lips to his and kissed him with my hands in his. He felt warm and alive. Soon our tender kiss became more fervent. He was the first to break contact.

"Wow," he said. "That's some thank-you."

"Too much?" I asked with an embarrassed smile. "If so, I blame it on the concussion."

"It's not too much." He kissed me again, and I snuggled up next to him. "We should probably go inside. What is this you want to show me? Something about a game?"

"Yeah, I saw Jeopardy hide it under the stairs." I slid out of the truck and closed the door behind me. Summerleigh looked like such an innocent place, but it was all an illusion. "You think Ben was right? That this place had activity before Summerleigh was built? That this property was haunted from the beginning?"

"I don't know how much stock I'd put in any of Ben's stories. I know he loved Harper and she trusted him for some reason, but he's not quite all there. I have heard about the other house, but like I said, the names of those people are lost at this point."

We walked into the house, and for the hundredth time, I surveyed the place. Even though there wasn't a stick of furniture in the Great Room, the smell of new wood encouraged me and reminded me that we were making progress. We were making a difference. One day, Summerleigh would be beautiful again, and she would be my own.

"Over here, Jesse. I didn't even notice this section of wall before. I mean, I looked at it but never noticed it. See how the panel is hidden in the grooves?" I waved him to the staircase and squatted down to get a good look at the hidden panel. Sure enough, it was right there.

"I never saw it either. But Summerleigh is huge, and I was so focused on the stairs and floor that I didn't think to look for a hidey hole." He squatted down beside me. "You say Jeopardy hid something in there?"

"Hidey hole?" I laughed. "I've never heard of that before."

"Must be a local thing. All good southern homes have hidey holes. It's where you keep the real important stuff."

"Like the family jewels?"

"No, like the moonshine. Or your mother-in-law's body. I'll have to tell you about that sometime. So what is it you think is in there? A game?"

My head throbbed, but I stayed focused. "Yes, a board game. Jeopardy and Marisol were playing with it. Jeopardy tucked a book inside of it. She showed it to me."

Jesse pushed on the panel, which came off surprisingly easily. He grinned at me, and I couldn't hide my enthusiasm. "Hey, do you have your phone?" I asked. He eased the panel to the side and dug his phone out of his pocket. Hitting the flashlight app, he illuminated the small space.

"I see a stack of games, and there's some other stuff too, a metal box and something else. Is that an old hat box? Can you hold the phone?" I did as he asked, and soon Jesse handed me a small stack of old games including Monopoly, Life and a box of playing cards.

They were covered in a layer of dust, but I didn't let that deter me. I opened the Life game and sorted through the pieces. There was no sign of the book. I dumped the box out, and the book fell into my lap. Jeopardy had tucked it under the insert.

Jesse was amazed at our discovery. "Hey, this book looks familiar. Like it belongs with the other one. See the cover? It's similar to the one you found in the potting shed."

I flipped it open, and my eyes fell on a familiar name, Jameson McIntyre. "Oh my gosh! Look at this, Jesse." I handed the book to him. He strained to read the text without his glasses since it was getting darker by the minute in here. I didn't hear the usual footsteps, but you never felt alone at Summerleigh. "Why don't we take all this stuff to the cottage and go through it there?"

"Okay. You got that stack?" We hurried back out of the house and headed to the cottage. Jesse grabbed his glasses from the truck, and then we went inside to examine our find. "No way was that a coincidence. You really did see Jeopardy Belle, Jerica."

"I told you I did. Don't tell me you didn't believe me," I said as I reached for a cloth to wipe the dust off the games. Once again we were huddled together around the kitchen table.

"I'm not saying that..." He opened the metal box but then paused and said, "Maybe that is what I meant. All this is new to me. I have always loved history, but to have it come to life...I'm not good at processing all this. There's no denying that Summerleigh is haunted. But to have a ghost tell you where something is hidden and have it be true isn't something you hear about every day. Look, I believe you, Jerica, but I have a scientist's mind. If I didn't, I wouldn't be here. No matter how attractive you are."

If he thought an offhand compliment would melt my heart, he had another thing coming. I thought he was attractive too, but I wasn't the girl next door. I was a strong woman with my nursing degree, which

I'd used to build a successful career. I wasn't some fawning teenager. I didn't say anything else for a minute or two. I picked up the book and opened it, carefully flipping through the pages. "I know you love Summerleigh. You have loved it for a long time, haven't you?"

He put the box down and examined the lock, which seemed to be rusted shut. "You know I wrote a book about the history of the house, about the Belle and McIntyre families. I hope you don't believe I'm here looking for material to write a new book. I think I'm done with writing books for a while. I have a few extras if you'd like one," he joked, but then his voice got serious again. "I mean it. I enjoy working in the house. It makes me feel connected to the people there. You have to admit they were interesting people. And bringing Jeopardy home, that meant something to me."

"Yeah, me too."

"I like you, Jerica Poole. I'm glad you're here."

"I like you, too. I'm glad you are here." I studied the book, still confused by the unfamiliar notations. At least I didn't have to strain to read them, even if I didn't understand them. The book had been well preserved in Jeopardy's hiding place.

"What in the world is this?" Jesse dumped out a bundle of strange braids and stacks of leather-bound books. He flipped open one of the books and whispered, "These are the lost books. These used to belong to John Jeffrey Belle. They're all about the McIntyre family. I knew it was true!"

"Get out of here! Really?"

"Yes, look. Here's his name. And this, this is all his research. Remember when I told you how obsessed he'd become with this place? Man, the answers we need about the boy might all be right here."

Looking at it with wide eyes, I added, "And Jeopardy wanted us to find this. She needed us to know. I think...I think she needs our help, Jesse. We have to help the ghosts of Summerleigh find peace with one another. This boy has to go. At least I know Jeopardy is staying close to Marisol. But where are John Jeffrey Belle and Harper?"

"They're at peace now, Jerica. They accomplished what they needed to do. Why would they be here?"

"But that means Jeopardy isn't at peace. She hasn't moved on. What have we missed?"

Jesse's face said it all. He knew the answer, and so did I. Jeopardy had been reunited with her father, that's true, but she didn't move on with him. Not yet. She wasn't resting with him. She had someone to look out for, someone to protect. Someone to watch over.

*Marisol! Jeopardy was protecting Marisol!*

Jeopardy Belle hadn't left Summerleigh because Marisol was here and the boy, the one with the black eyes, was too strong for my daughter. He would keep her away from me forever if he could.

"Jeopardy!" I gasped as the thoughts came together like puzzle pieces in my mind. "Jeopardy is here for Marisol." I started to shake. "Oh, Jesse. We have to find out who he is. We have to get the paranormal team back here."

Jesse was on his feet as quick as lightning. "We'll do it, Jerica. We'll do it, I swear. Let me get you your blanket. Your teeth are chattering." He raced out of the room to fetch my favorite throw blanket with the pink roses on it.

And then I saw the boy, reflected in the glass of the china cabinet. I turned around, but he wasn't there. No, he wasn't there anymore, but he had been. And he knew what we were trying to do.

*Oh, Marisol. Sweetheart! Stay close to Jeopardy! Mommy is coming soon. I promise.*

## Chapter Fifteen—Harper

As I expected, Addison wouldn't wake up. "Get up, Addie. It's going to be light out soon, and we want to get to the river before sunup."

"It's too early, and my stomach hurts."

"Your stomach hurts because you need to eat something. You never eat anymore. Please, Addie. I have a basket of food. I baked us some blueberry muffins last night while Momma was at the Ladies Auxiliary. Come with me. Spending time in the sunshine would do you good, Addison. You'll feel better. I'll bait all your hooks for you. Don't make me go by myself, please."

It wasn't that I was afraid to go alone. Ben was nothing to be afraid of, but I didn't want to be alone with anyone, not if I thought they liked me. And I was pretty sure he did. I didn't like him like Jeopardy liked Troy. I wasn't opposed to having a friend who was a boy, but I would rather there be no confusion about my feelings. I had no intention of giving my heart away so easily, and certainly not to a boy who was younger than me.

"No, Harper. Now let me sleep."

I sighed in exasperation. I hated leaving her here by herself. What if Momma's mood took a turn? There would be no one to help Addison fend her off. But there wasn't anything I could do about it, and a promise was a promise. I had told Ben I would go fishing, and I tried to keep my word. He was my friend, after all.

To avoid any misunderstanding, I left a note for Momma on the kitchen table explaining where I was going and who I would be with. If she wanted to, she could ride down to Dog River and find me. We planned on fishing off the bank near the road. I'd be able to see her coming because there were no trees there.

I'd managed to rig Daddy's old fishing pole, and I did a pretty good job if I did say so myself. I'd left it by the potting shed along with the tackle box. I'd been willing to share all my goodies with Addison, but since she wanted to be Sleeping Beauty this morning, she'd just miss out on the fun. I snapped my fingers when I remembered I'd left my fishing hat in my bedroom. It was one of Daddy's that I'd found in a chest in Jeopardy's castle room. I'd raced up there yesterday to get it and saw nary a ghost. I couldn't believe my luck. I tiptoed back down the hall to my bedroom.

I heard Momma giggling and then a man's voice. There was a man in Momma's room, and he would be coming out soon. I could hear them both laughing, and he was saying things no man should say to a respectable lady. I pulled my hat down on my head to cover my ears and hurried out of the house. I was tempted to linger outside to see who Momma was entertaining, but I needn't have bothered. Dewey Landry had never been that smart. His parked truck was halfway hidden in the wild woods next to our house.

She was disgusting! Right here in our own house? What would Mr. Daughdrill say about that? I had a mind to tell Aunt Dot right this minute if I could get her on the phone. Maybe I'd steal Dewey's truck and drive it over to her house.

Feeling sick to my stomach now, I munched an apple to save the muffin for Ben. I walked down the gravel pathway and made a quick stop by the potting shed to retrieve my fishing pole and tackle box. Then I continued on to Dog River, relieved that I wouldn't have to hear Momma pretending to be a lady this morning. I expected to see Ben there when I got there, but he wasn't.

*This had been his idea; he better not cut out on me. I have better things to do with my Saturdays*, I lied to myself like I was someone important.

He was supposed to bring the worms, but after an hour I realized he wasn't coming. I used my apple core as bait but didn't catch a thing and succeeded only in losing the core. I had no shovel for digging up worms and no idea where to look for them anyway. I mean, I knew they were in the dirt, but according to Ben, worms liked certain types of soil. He should know—his older brother ran a bait business down at the Escatawpa. About ten o'clock, I decided to go home. Ben had stood me up, and we hadn't even been on a date. I put Daddy's pole and tackle box back in the potting shed. I'd try again later, even if I had to get my own bait.

*I'd better go check on Addie.*

I went inside and was amazed to find that Addison and Momma both were still in bed. Now Momma, I could understand. She'd been carousing all night; that's what Daddy accused her of once. I didn't know the exact definition of "carousing," but I was pretty sure it meant acting like a floozy. Momma used to call Jeopardy a floozy all the time.

I wasn't home ten minutes when George County's youngest deputy, Andrew Hayes, arrived at our doorstep. I touched my hair to make sure my bob was in place, but I could tell that this would be no pleasant visit. Sheriff Passeau—I remembered to call him Sheriff and not Deputy, since he'd just been promoted—was here too, and both men were holding their hats in their hands.

That was always a bad sign.

I opened the door and waited to hear the news. Had they actually found Jeopardy? Or had something happened to Aunt Dot and Loxley? Last I heard, Loxley had the chicken pox and had been out of school for nearly two weeks. Momma called daily, but Aunt Dot refused to bring her home. I was forbidden to call, but I'd already made up my mind to disobey Momma in this.

Now it might be too late. "May I help you, Deputy? Sheriff?"

Deputy Hayes' expression saddened. "I'm afraid we have some bad news, Miss Belle. We need to speak to your mother."

I opened the door and invited them into the Great Room. "I'll get her for you. I think she's lying down. She and Addison have been under the weather. Please excuse me."

"Thank you, Miss Belle," the deputy whispered to me as my face flushed. I nodded once and left the room and hurried to Momma's side.

"Momma, you have to get up. The sheriff and the deputy are here to see you. I think something bad has happened."

To my surprise, Momma wasn't sleeping. She was just lying there staring off into space. "What did you do, Jeopardy?" I could barely hear her whisper.

"I'm Harper, Momma. Please get dressed and come see the sheriff. Let me help you. You can't go in there in your slip."

"Get out, Harper. I'll dress myself, if you please," she snapped as she crawled out of her tangled sheets.

"I'll tell them you are coming."

I raced to Addison's room and woke her up. She immediately got up and got dressed. Apparently, she too believed there was big news. Had to be. Why else would they be here?

A few minutes later, Momma strutted into the Great Room with a lit skinny cigarette in her hand. These past few weeks had taken a toll on her elegance, but she was still a pretty woman. And even though she'd been misbehaving just a few hours ago, she was acting as polite as the Queen of England now.

"Would you like something to drink? Maybe some iced tea or coffee? Harper, where are your manners? Please, gentlemen, come sit in the parlor." They obeyed, but I made no move to put coffee on.

"Ma'am, we are here at the coroner's request," Sheriff Passeau said.

Momma's hand flew to her throat, and she gasped. I knew immediately that something was wrong. Momma could pose as pretty as any catalog model, but she was a horrible actor. I was convinced that whatever she was about to hear would come as no surprise to her.

"Ma'am, your father is dead. He was found this morning at his home in Barton. His housekeeper discovered him in his bed."

"What?" Momma said quietly. So this wasn't what she expected to hear after all. She thought they were going to tell her something else.

*Like what? What did she expect to hear?* My stomach soured, and Addison sank down onto the couch beside Momma. Of all the people in the world, Addison may have been the only one who cared about Mr. Daughdrill.

"I'm sorry to say he did not die of natural causes," Deputy Hayes said discreetly, "but you don't have to see him. The housekeeper gave a positive identification when we arrived. I think that's good enough for us, and we all know Mr. Daughdrill."

"How?" I asked, uncaring if I sounded morbid or not.

"He was stabbed multiple times in the chest," Sheriff Passeau said, placing his steely gaze on me. "With a pair of shears, presumably while he slept since there was no sign of a struggle. While nothing appears to be missing, we thought maybe you could come and check his property, Mrs. Belle. We may have missed something."

Momma rubbed her face with her pale hands. She looked very confused. "You say my father? My father is dead? He has been murdered?"

Passeau answered, "Yes, ma'am. He's dead." He glanced at the deputy as if to say something in their secret police language. I wished I knew it.

Momma stood to her feet slowly, and I thought she would fall over. Maybe she would faint. To my horror, she began to scream and sob, which made Addison do the same. And Momma didn't scream once but over and over again. No amount of talking to her would make her stop sobbing. And when she was done sobbing, she began to laugh and talk to herself.

Deputy Hayes said, "I'll send for a doctor, Miss Belle. She's going to need a sedative. You should call your aunt and ask her to come help with her."

The deputy had a point, but I didn't think Aunt Dot would pick up the phone. And then it occurred to me. Momma did expect something to happen. She'd prepared for it, daydreamed about it all morning. But this wasn't it. What, then? Suddenly, I worried for Aunt Dot. It was no secret that the Daughdrill sisters had tied up over Loxley and that Momma was furious that Aunt Dot hadn't brought her baby home. There were things going on that I didn't understand. To top it all off, Momma had been entertaining Dewey Landry. No, I couldn't fathom any of this.

"Deputy Hayes, I think my aunt's phone is out of order. Once the doctor arrives and I get Momma settled, would you mind taking me over there? I would like her to hear the news from one of us, if you please."

"Of course I will. Always happy to help a lady."

Addison was sitting with Momma now. Momma had her head on Addison's shoulder, looking at something none of us could see. Sheriff Passeau spoke kindly to her, which was something of a rarity for him. She continued to sob, her face a mess now with streaking black mascara and tear-stained powder. Soon, Dr. Leland arrived at the house with his black bag. With his encouragement, Momma went to bed and took a tranquilizer that would help her sleep. He left me a bottle of about ten more and warned me not to let her have the bottle.

"People experiencing grief do the unpredictable, young lady. See that you give her only one at a time, and only twice a day. I'll come back if you need me."

He patted my shoulder kindly and left Summerleigh. He'd always been our biggest peach customer.

"I'll be right back, Addie. I promise." I kissed her cheek and noticed that she had stopped crying and hadn't said much at all. I worried about leaving her, but Momma couldn't be by herself right now.

Deputy Hayes pulled out all the stops for me. He used his siren and horn to get us to Aunt Dot's in no time. To my surprise, we weren't the first people there. A repairman was cutting out wood for a broken window. Aunt Dot ran to me and hugged me.

"What happened?" the deputy and I asked at the same time.

"Someone tried to break into the house this morning, not that long ago. I guess that's what he was trying to do. He shot my bedroom window all up." Her hands were shaking when she held mine. "Your sister slept through the whole thing."

"That sounds like Loxley," I said with a small smile. "I am sorry to come here like this, but I have more bad news to tell you."

"What is it, Harper? Is it Jeopardy?"

"No, ma'am. It's Mr. Daughdrill. He died sometime this morning. Someone killed him, Aunt Dot. In his own bed."

She sank slowly into her cane-back kitchen chair. "Any suspects, Deputy?"

"No, ma'am. We're just beginning our investigation, and with what happened to you, I'm even more concerned. Do you know anyone who might want to harm you? Someone who might want to kill you?"

Aunt Dot looked at me; her heart-shaped face was sad and kind of broken. "I never think about those things, Deputy. I wouldn't want to make a list like that."

"Well, I think you should come with us. Your sister is beside herself with grief."

Aunt Dot stood up and put her glass in the sink. "No, I don't think I will. And believe me, sir, my sister has all the comfort she needs now. Harper, tell Addison I will come see y'all soon."

"Ma'am, I don't think you understand. Mrs. Belle had to be given a sedative, and these young ladies are by themselves."

Aunt Dot brushed away a tear but shook her head stubbornly. "I'm sorry. I have to think about Loxley."

I looked at the deputy. "May I have one more minute? In private, Deputy Hayes."

"Yes, but I have to get back to the precinct after I take you home. We've got a lot going on today, Miss Belle." He shot Aunt Dot one last look of disapproval and walked out on the porch.

I turned to Aunt Dot. "May I see Loxley a minute? Is she feeling better?"

She smiled and accepted the tissue I offered her. "She's not contagious now. Of course you can see her. Her scabs are healing, and the doctor says she won't have any scars at all."

Just then, my sister walked into the kitchen, looking confused at all the hubbub going on around her. Aunt Dot said sweetly, "Loxley, look who's here."

"Harper!" She raced toward me with her black and white stuffed pony in her hands. We hugged, and I cried; I was so happy to see my baby sister. "Guess what?"

"What?" I asked.

She whispered in my ear, "I don't wet the bed anymore. There aren't any ghosts here."

"That is wonderful, Loxley. That means you're all grown up now. You'll be driving a car soon and getting a job as the world's stuffed animal zookeeper."

She laughed and said, "Do they have that?"

"No, silly. They don't."

"Then I'll be the first."

I hugged her again. "I have to go home now, but I'll come back to see you again soon. I promise."

She poked her lip out but didn't complain. She wanted to show me her room and all her dresses, but I had to leave. I couldn't stay another moment or I'd never want to return to Summerleigh. Aunt

Dot's small cottage was so peaceful and quiet. You could feel the love in this place. I kissed them both and ran out of the house crying. This was what love felt like.

Accepting, healing and peaceful.

One day, if I was lucky, I'd have that kind of love too.

## *Chapter Sixteen—Harper*

Momma wasn't going to be happy unless she was the center of attention at her own father's funeral. The First Baptist Church of Desire, Mississippi, turned out in a big way. Although Mr. Daughdrill didn't attend church regularly, he frequently pledged money to special causes like the girls' choir. He bought all their robes last year and even paid for their trip to Tennessee to sing at the Baptist Convention up there.

Oh yes, Mr. Daughdrill was something of a big deal in this community...still, there were whispers in between the speeches and testimonials about the fine citizen they were laying to rest. Since I was so plain and quiet, people talked in front of me like I wasn't even there.

*Well, there was that time he'd been involved with that one incident.*

*Remember when he was asked about that girl?*

*Oh, that was so long ago, and he was young himself then.*

*No, his granddaughter. They questioned him about Jeopardy.*

*Oh, yes, they did. I heard it from...*

And then the conversation broke off because the next person took the podium to make glowing statements about Mr. Daughdrill, a man many people secretly hated.

Momma had borrowed the fold-up chairs from the church and had them arranged in the Great Room. We'd lit the fireplace to make it look nice in here, even though it was as hot as Hades. I opened the back door to let some of the heat out. Even Mr. Daughdrill's makeup looked a bit shiny, as if it would slide off his face at any moment. Why she had to bring him here, I had no idea.

I stood in the back of the room near the open door drinking my soda through a straw when Aunt Dot came in with Loxley by her side. I'd refused to pay my respects and walk by his casket pretending to miss him. I'm sure Momma wasn't pleased with me, but I didn't care. I didn't want to see him again, and I was glad he was gone. I would have preferred a more peaceful death for him, but that was beyond my control.

Like Momma, Addison was dressed to the nines. She wore her shoulder-length hair pulled back in a ribbon and wore a dark blue dress with black sleeves. Such a stylish dress for someone so young. She placed a white rose on Mr. Daughdrill's chest and walked away.

She seemed to genuinely miss him, which gave me some relief. If he'd behaved inappropriately with her, she wouldn't be acting this way. She wouldn't be acting as if she had just lost the grandfather she loved. No, his death came at the right time. I don't know how I knew all this, but I did. Call it a young woman's intuition if you like.

Ben caught me at the door after the service. "Hey, I'm sorry about your grandfather, Harper." He stuck out his hand like he was meeting me for the first time. I couldn't help but notice it was bandaged up. Like he'd been in a fight with someone.

"What happened to you, Ben? You didn't show up for fishing, and you look like you put your hand in a wood chipper. Is it serious?"

"Did you say he put his hand in a wood chipper?" Addie joined us, chewing on a celery stick and smiling at Ben. She was clearly interested in talking with him, which suited me fine. I was still ticked off that he'd stood me up for our fishing date. Well, not date. I wasn't interested in dating Ben.

"No, that's not what happened. Excuse me. Hey, wait, Harper. Don't run off. I need to talk to you."

"Okay, so talk." I was getting anxious because I wanted to spend time with Aunt Dot and Loxley.

"Well, I can't talk to you here. Come outside. It won't take but a minute."

I tucked my cardigan around me and arranged my barrettes. I needed a haircut in the worst sort of way.

Once we got outside, Ben said, "I've been meaning to tell you this for a very long time, Harper Belle. I know you barely know me, and you probably didn't realize that we've been in school together for almost two years."

"Really? Has it been that long?" *I really wish he would get to the point.*

"I mean to say, I know I'm young. And I know you're young. We're both young." Ben's dithering was getting on my nerves. And it was hot out here.

"Spit it out, Ben Hartley. We are at my grandfather's funeral."

He glanced around him and saw that a few people were looking in our direction. *Well, if he didn't want to be embarrassed, he shouldn't make a fool of himself.*

"What I am trying to say is that I love you, Harper. I have always loved you. And I hope you know I would do anything for you," he said, showing me his hands and looking at me with a serious expression, "and I do mean anything. Don't let my size fool you, because I got a heart as big as any other guy. And that heart loves you, Harper Belle." He took my hand and kissed it as if he was a knight and I was his lady. It was the most ridiculous thing I had ever seen.

I pulled back my hand and felt my cheeks redden to the shade of a vine-ripe tomato. I said, "Please, Ben. Go home." I paid no attention to the small gathering that had begun to watch us and even applaud. There was the tittering of laughter from some of the older women and good-natured guffawing from some of the men. Ben sputtered in frustration. Obviously, things had not gone the way he had planned them. He cast an evil eye my direction and stormed off the porch and down Hurlette Drive. I wasn't going to chase him. I had no idea where he was going. I resolved that I wouldn't go fishing with Ben Hartley, or any other boy I wasn't serious about, ever again.

"Not even eighteen years old and already breaking hearts," Deputy Hayes said politely.

"Oh, he's just a friend. Thanks for coming to the service." The deputy looked so much nicer today than when he wore his brown uniform. I liked him in blue. "It means a lot."

He ducked his head and walked away with a smile.

Aunt Dot appeared out of the crowd and hugged my neck. "He's right, you know. You're as lovely as your Momma."

"Bite your tongue, Aunt Dot. I don't want to be anything like her." I glanced in Momma's direction. She was sitting in the red velvet chair receiving a line of guests with a distressed look on her face. She caught me looking, but I quickly looked back at Aunt Dot. "I would give anything for you to be my mother."

Aunt Dot sighed and kissed Loxley on the forehead before she ran to our mother, who scooped her up in her arms and made a big deal of her. Loxley sat proudly in her lap as the mourners came forward and expressed their condolences to our family.

"Once upon a time, I would have scolded you for saying such things, but now I understand a little better. Having Loxley with me, I learned a few things. Your little sister is much more observant than you might believe. I was astonished to hear some of the things she told me. I'm sorry for all you had to go through, Harper. I want to make amends, if you'll let me. I want to make it up to you and Addison. You had to endure so much with no help from anyone, but that's going to change."

"You can't change it, Aunt Dot. No more than I can. All we can be is who we are. All we can do is play the roles that are assigned to us. We are not in control of our destinies."

She hugged me up and whispered in my ear, "I hope you don't believe that. I hope you never believe that. You have choices in life. I know things seem hopeless right now because you're young and still living at home, but that's not forever. It is gonna get better. As a matter of fact, I want you and Addison to come and live with me. I will make a home for us; we'll make one together. And I have it on good authority that neither your mother nor I will ever have to worry about money again. Your grandfather was generous to us at least at his death. You girls can go to any college you want, be anything you want to be. I will make sure it happens for you. Just come with me." Addison had joined us and leaned her head on Aunt Dot's shoulder even though she was much taller than our aunt. It was an awkward but sweet picture. And then Loxley came running to us, and I scooped her up in my arms and held her tight. I smelled her fresh, clean hair and her naturally vanilla scent.

"She'll never let me go, Aunt Dot. You know that."

And then Momma started to cry. She was standing by Mr. Daughdrill's coffin now, looking down at him holding his cold dead hand in hers. "Poppa, Poppa why did you leave me?" She cried and wailed and nearly fainted until someone helped her into the kitchen for a cup of coffee.

Soon, Miss Augustine barreled in my direction. "There you are. I've been looking everywhere for you, Harper Louise. Your mother is beside herself with grief. The least you could do is show some compassion. If you don't come now, I don't know what we're going to do with her."

Aunt Dot replied, "She'll be right there, Augustine."

Miss Augustine appeared to have a smart reply right on the tip of her tongue, but I waved my hand at her. "Tell Momma I'll be right there."

Aunt Dot held my hands and ignored Loxley's whining. "You don't have to do this, Harper. You do not owe her anything. She has it all wrong. She owes you everything."

I sighed, and my soul felt like a heavy anchor. "Without me here, I don't know what she'll do. She won't have anyone. She drinks all the time now. Until today, she wasn't even talking to Miss Augustine. She doesn't go to the movies anymore. And you know about the other things."

My aunt's eyes widened for a moment, and she nodded her head. "But you can't fix it, Harper. Someone else will step up into your place. Someone else will have to pacify her. You've done enough. I've already lost one of you girls because I waited too long. I can't lose another one. I love you all so much. Please come with me, Harper and Addison. Loxley wants to stay, and she wants her sisters with her."

With all my heart, I wanted to say yes. A part of me said, *Go now and pack your bag!* But I couldn't. Things had happened that I just didn't understand, and I needed to understand them. I needed to know how those scissors made it to my grandfather's house, for I felt sure it was no coincidence that he'd been stabbed to death with a pair of silver scissors. Had that spirit killed him? The little boy with the black eyes? And why did Momma act so strange when we got the news that Grandfather was dead? No, I couldn't leave yet.

The other shoe hadn't dropped yet. But it would. For now, I would stay with Momma. But knowing that I had options, that I had somewhere to go, set me free.

I would stay with her for a little while, but I would never again be her prisoner.

Never again.

## *Chapter Seventeen—Jerica*

I rolled over in my bed and reached for Marisol's stuffed animal. It wasn't there. It must have fallen off the nightstand. I probably bumped it sometime during the night...I've been told I'm a wild sleeper. And I apparently snore. At some point, I'd have to search through my old albums to find a good picture of her and buy a nice frame, but I wasn't ready to do that yet. It was easier to not remember those lost moments.

"Good morning, Marisol," I whispered. The sunlight streamed into my room from the open window. Of course, I heard nothing and never would, but I couldn't spend the morning wallowing in self-pity. Hannah and her friends were coming this afternoon, and I had a whole host of chores to get done before then. My head didn't hurt too bad, and thinking about all the things that could have gone horribly wrong, I considered myself extremely lucky to have woken up this morning.

And then I thought about Harper. She had loved my daughter just like she was her own grandchild. At least I was still connected to Harper in some strange way. I never knew she'd had such a horrible up-bringing, but it felt good to know she eventually had choices.

Poor Ben. I felt embarrassed for him, but he'd been young and in love...still, who tells someone that you love them at a funeral? He and Harper had apparently worked through that bit of awkwardness because he had been a dear friend of hers later in life, at least according to him. I still thought it was strange that she never spoke about him or mentioned him to me in the years that we'd known one another. I guess that proved relationships were complicated no matter what decade or century you were in.

I got busy tidying the house and doing mundane things like taking out the trash and mopping the kitchen floor, things I had neglected to do for the past week. How was I going to let the reconstruction crew back into the house knowing that I might put them in danger? I'd canceled work for today, but I couldn't leave the guys hanging forever. Seriously, I had to put an end to this—get to the bottom of who this kid was and get him out of Summerleigh. Not just for me but for everyone.

Time flew by, and soon I had guests arriving at the house. I was happy that Jesse was there first. Renee wasn't going to make it because she had some problem at the diner; since we didn't have to wait for her, we quickly got into his latest finds. I'd allowed him to take John Jeffrey Belle's research home, and by the looks of him, he'd pulled an all-nighter examining the material.

"This guy, this Jameson McIntyre, he was one troubled individual. It's a good thing his father got him out of Desire before the law caught up with him because I'd say he was the obvious choice for a suspect. He had this weird fetish, Jerica. He liked cutting things."

"You mean like stabbing people? I think there is a name for that."

"Up until the murder of his sister, there's nothing to indicate that Jameson McIntyre went around stabbing people, but he did like to keep souvenirs." Jesse put the box on the table and dug out the journal we found in the Life board game, the one Jeopardy showed me. "See, I figured it out. These notations aren't locations or clues to anything. They're just a record of his sick victories. For instance, beside the name Claudette, you see the abbreviation HR? It stands for hair. He cut this girl's hair. And over here, this abbreviation? RB? That stands for ribbon."

"I can't believe this. You're right, he was sick. But I thought you said Jameson was much older than the boy we saw. I mean, why would his younger brother be popping up everywhere if it's Jameson's malicious spirit wreaking havoc on the other ghosts of Summerleigh?"

Jesse put the journal back into the box and closed it. "All good questions, and I have no answers. Maybe Hannah's friends can help us. They should be here any minute. But thanks to John Jeffrey Belle, we have a lot more information than we did. He really took meticulous notes. Oh, I forgot..." He opened the box again and removed a small bundle. "Don't read this now. But when you get a chance later, I think you should check it out. It might explain a few things."

I accepted the packet of faded letters and ran my finger over the pale pink ribbon that tied them together. How could I resist diving into these now? I caught my breath when I saw the top envelope. It was addressed to Dorothy Daughdrill. I had no time to ask questions because there was a knock on the front door. No doubt it was Hannah, right on time as usual. I welcomed her crew in, and we shared with them the information that Jesse had just presented to me. I took a minute to deposit the envelopes in my nightstand drawer and raced back downstairs to lead the crew into Summerleigh.

"Wow, this place is amazing." Rex took a minute to take in his surroundings. He clearly appreciated all the work we'd been doing in the house.

"It's huge. How many square feet is this?" Amy asked.

"You know, I'm not really sure. With the upstairs and everything, probably close to 5,000. Maybe more. I know it's a lot of house to cover, but most of the activity happens on the second floor and in and around the attic."

"It's a good thing too because I only have four cameras with me. I'll make it work," she said good-naturedly as she carried cases up the stairs. While Amy set up cameras on the second floor, I showed Hannah the collection of books we'd found, the ones that John Jeffrey Belle used to write down the clues he'd found about the Lady in White and her potential killer. According to the journals, John Belle had seen the ghosts on several occasions and tried to communicate with them but had no luck. Hannah pointed out that there wasn't much in the way of paranormal investigation techniques in those days. Ghost hunting had not gone mainstream, and the chances that he could communicate directly with the spirits without some of these new devices were slim.

Jesse said, "It really frustrated him because he wanted to help Mariana McIntyre. He'd even considered holding a séance upstairs but didn't get around to it as far as I could tell. He died unexpectedly, as you know." Hannah nodded and began walking around the room, her favorite purse on her arm, as he continued, "From what John wrote, Mariana was a lot more active back when the Belles were here. And even then she wasn't harming anyone."

"She pushed Ann Belle down the stairs, Jesse."

"You saw her push someone?" Rex asked with some surprise.

I thought about it a moment. "Not exactly. More like she scared her so badly that she fell down the stairs. Broke her arm, but it stopped her from beating on Jeopardy."

Jesse said, "Mariana used to appear downstairs when the Belles first moved in here. She was often seen crying in the Great Room and said the name Jameson repeatedly. It's almost like she was a residual haunt but eventually retreated to the upstairs. I guess that would also make her an intelligent haunt."

"Sounds like you know a little bit about paranormal investigation," Rex said, grinning at Jesse.

Jesse shook his head and said, "Only what I've seen on TV. I'll leave that stuff to you guys."

"Hey!" Amy called from upstairs. "Can you guys come up here a minute?"

Alarmed, we hurried up the stairs and followed Amy's voice to the nursery. "What is it? Did you see something?" Hannah asked.

"No, but is that supposed to be here?"

I couldn't believe it. Marisol's purple bear was hanging from the broken light. Someone had tied a string around the toy's neck and strung it up there. It couldn't have been easy to do—the ceilings were eight feet tall.

"That's my baby's toy. I had it in my room on my nightstand."

"That can't be good," Amy said dryly as she walked over to it and pointed her flashlight up at it. "I want to take some readings before we take it down. Hey, Rex, would you mind getting the EMF detector? It's in my case right there."

"Sure."

I hovered in the doorway as they waved their equipment around the bear. They were apparently disappointed in the readings, and Amy declared it a mystery.

"Someone, a living someone, could have done this, you know. Does anyone else have keys to this place?" Amy asked as she and Rex worked to get the bear down from the light with the ladder Jesse had brought from the kitchen. She handed the bear back to me, and I shook my head.

"Who would do that? Nobody has keys to this place except Jesse and me. And he didn't know anything about that bear, what it signifies or who it belonged to. That was my daughter's toy. I keep it close, like I said, on my nightstand because..."

"You don't have to explain why you keep that." Hannah touched my shoulder gently, and I clutched the bear to my chest. Amy set up a camera in the corner of the room and asked a few more questions, and then the five of us headed to the attic.

Rex visibly shuddered as he approached the door. "Sheesh, it's cold up here. Heat normally rises. Who's got a thermometer?"

Amy tapped on her phone and handed it to him. "You know I have every paranormal investigation app there is. Try this one." She stepped inside and wandered around.

Hannah seemed hesitant about joining us but eventually did. "It feels so different now. Not like the last time. I do feel like there is some sort of battle going on here. Young and old. That's what I keep hearing, young and old." She wandered around, staring at the walls, the ceilings and the many nooks and crannies in the attic. Then she squatted down in front of a familiar chest, the one that Loxley had discovered. She opened it and immediately rocked back on her heels. "Oh my. Such a sweet presence. Such a sweet girl. She didn't deserve what happened to her. She never expected that he would hurt her. She loved him, and he turned on her. She never expected it."

I looked at Jesse, unsure how to process what was happening. Still clutching the bear, I hung back and listened. Rex leaned over to me and said, "This is a good thing. She's tuning in. That means the spirits are talking to her." I wanted to say to him, "I know what that means," but I kept my mouth shut and my eyes open. I had learned from experience, both mine and Harper's, that you could take nothing for granted in this attic.

Hannah was on her feet and pacing around the attic. "He doesn't like people being in here. He has a treasure somewhere here." She waved at a wall and then kept pacing up and down the floor. "No, he doesn't. His buried treasure is here. He says the girls were too nosy. They like to plunder and look through his things, but those are his treasures." Hannah's hand flew to her heart, and she gasped in surprise. "He inherited those treasures. When his brother left, he gave them to him. They are precious to him. He doesn't want us here. We have to go! I think he's coming!"

Jesse put his arm around me protectively, and we all waited as if the boy would step into the room. Did they understand what this meant? The boy wasn't the one who killed Mariana! It was his brother—it was most certainly Jameson—but the boy wasn't leaving. Not without his treasure.

"What is his name, Hannah? We need his name," I reminded her in a whisper. But Hannah didn't move. She stared at the window over the place where Jeopardy used to sleep. "Hannah?"

"In the hallway. I'm hearing footsteps. Anyone else?" Amy retrieved her camera from somewhere and began filming the session. She nodded her head at Rex, and I strained to hear what they were talking about. It didn't take but a few seconds. Yes, there were definitely footsteps, and they were walking toward the attic. I took a step back, and Jesse came with me. Amy, Rex and Hannah did not move. I expected the door to slam, as they did so frequently on this floor, but nothing happened. The footsteps stopped outside the door, and still we waited. It would be completely dark in here soon, and I didn't fancy the idea of hanging out in this attic in the darkness. The room felt very different from the other day when Marisol and Jeopardy were playing their game. It had felt light and sunny, warm and inviting. Now, not so much.

And that's when I heard the whisper.

*Run, pie-face!*

# *Chapter Eighteen—Jerica*

"Jerica!" Jesse called me as I snatched him by the hand and ran out of the attic. As soon as my foot hit the top step of the staircase, I felt a blast of cold air. "Jerica, wait!" Jesse pulled me close.

"We have to go. I heard Jeopardy's voice. She told me to run. You didn't hear her?" The rest of the team filtered out of the attic and joined us in the hallway. Jesse didn't have a chance to answer me. One of the devices that Amy deployed in the nursery was making a whirring sound. As the three of them entered the room, Jesse held me tight.

"We can get out of here if you want. They don't need us here to do what they're doing."

"No, I'm good." I stepped back and tucked my hair behind my ear. "But we had to get out of there." I could hear Hannah talking in the other room, and she wasn't talking to Amy or Rex. She was speaking to the boy. The hair on the back of my neck pricked up, and I froze as I listened to her. I didn't want to go into the nursery, not just yet. Jesse stood beside me as we heard her ask him to tell her his name.

"It's okay. We are not here to steal your treasure. We just want to know your name. We know your brother's name. Tell us your name." She whispered to Rex, "Do you have the audio recorder going?"

"Yes."

"We're not going to be here for much longer. You don't want to be forgotten, do you? You deserve to be remembered. Tell us your name and we will leave."

They waited a few more minutes, and I heard Amy say, "Let's play it back." I walked to the doorway but didn't go into the room. The atmosphere had shifted. It felt dark, even morose. I could plainly hear Hannah's voice on the recorder but nothing else. I heard her sigh.

"Any suggestions? He really doesn't want to talk." Rex sounded frustrated, which didn't encourage me. What if all I was doing was making things worse? What if Ben Hartley had been right? This suddenly seemed like a bad idea.

"Maybe we should try one of the other rooms. It looks like it's going to be a long night," Hannah answered, but she didn't sound dissuaded.

I was happy to leave them to their work because I was beginning to feel like I couldn't breathe. The air was so thick up here. Surely I wasn't the only one who noticed it. "Can we go downstairs? I'd like to get out of here for a little while."

Jesse agreed, and we walked down the stairs and left the paranormal investigators alone. Maybe they would have better luck without me around.

I paced around in the Great Room. I didn't want to leave Summerleigh; it would be irresponsible to leave people in here. I was the one who had suggested this, and I was going to see it through.

"You need anything, Jerica?"

Clutching the teddy bear, I shook my head. "No. I'm fine." I stopped pacing and stood beside him. "Thanks, Jesse." He hugged me briefly, and then it was his turn to pace the floor.

Then I heard the scratching sound. At first, I thought it might be a mouse or a rat scratching at some wood, but that wasn't quite it. And it was coming from the hallway that led to the bedrooms. I raised my eyebrows and looked at Jesse.

"Yeah, I'm hearing it too," he said. "Sounds like it's coming from in there."

"Should we go tell them?"

He shook his head and said, "No. I think we can handle this. Might just be a rodent."

"Okay." We headed toward the hallway as the scratching continued. It wasn't quite like a rodent, more like a smooth scratching sound. And it was coming from Addison and Loxley's bedroom. I knew that sound! I'd heard it before. Or at least Harper had. That was the sound of someone drawing with chalk on the floor.

Loxley! As we stepped into the room, I smelled the faint scent of vanilla. Yes, Loxley! It felt so much better in this room than upstairs.

"Look at that! Someone was just drawing in here. What does that say? You know I can't read without my glasses."

"It looks like 'Jacob.' Loxley did this...she gave us the answer we needed. That's his name—his name is Jacob!"

As soon as I said that, a loud thud smashed above us. "We have to go up there. We have to tell them." There was another thud, but not above us this time. The sound came from the wall. I didn't run or flinch. I walked out of Loxley's room, down the hallway and through the Great Room.

*I know your name now. You can't stay here. You can't torment us anymore, and you will not harm my daughter.*

Lightning illuminated the room in blue light. Thunder soon followed, and the house shook as if a sonic boom had crashed overhead. Jesse was right behind me, and we found the team in one of the other rooms.

"I know his name, and I know what we have to do," I said. I swallowed at the thought of facing off with this spirit again, but it had to be done. There was going to be peace in this house, one way or another. Time to let the ghosts of the past rest. Some part of me felt sorry for this boy, that he would inherit such a perverse treasure and that he would linger here long after his death to watch over it. Yes, I felt pity for him, and it grew stronger than my fear with every passing second. "Hannah, the boy's name is Jacob. He has to be Jameson and Mariana's younger brother. Loxley wrote his name on the floor downstairs." Thunder rolled over us, and the floor began to creak. Was it just the old house settling, or was something more ominous about to happen?

"That's great," she began as all the doors slammed shut at once. Even calm, cool and collected Amy jumped at the sound.

"He's here," I said as I held onto Marisol's bear with both hands.

"It's not going to be as simple as calling his name, not if he's attached to something in that attic. We need to find his treasure and move it. If we get it out of the house, he'll leave with it. We're going to need a distraction, though. Are you ready for this, Jerica?" Hannah asked with sincere concern. *What was she asking me?*

"Yes. What do we do?"

Hannah sent Jesse, Rex and Amy to the attic to search for Jameson's morbid collection. Jesse didn't want to leave me, but I assured him everything would be okay. "I'm in good hands."

The door opened without a fight. But when we entered the room, it closed behind us. And during the time my attention went from the door to the room, everything had changed. This wasn't an empty nursery anymore. There was a large, round blue carpet in the center of the floor. One large chair was positioned in front of the fireplace. Heavy blue curtains hung from the window, and there were three desks at the back of the room. I could see a large wooden toy box, a rocking horse and books that filled a bookcase I did not recognize.

"Hannah?" I whispered as she took my hand. "What's going on?"

"Talk to him, Jerica. I can't see what you're seeing, but I can feel him."

Talking to him was the last thing I wanted to do. He looked like something out of a horror movie with his white skin and black eyes. I couldn't see his face fully, but those horrible eyes were as plain as day. *How do you reason with something like this? Just kill some time, Jerica. Give them time.*

"I know your name now." The boy raised his head, and I swear I heard him growl. "My friend Loxley told me your name. She knows you. You used to play with her."

The rocking horse began to move back and forth, and the flames in the fireplace rose.

"My name is Jerica, and you're Jacob. I am not here to hurt you, Jacob."

"That's good. Keep talking, Jerica."

The horse rocked faster, and the clock on the mantelpiece began to make a horrible sound. I glanced at it and could see the hour and minute hands spinning wildly, like an unseen hand was manipulating them.

"Jacob, I know you want to stay here, but you can't. You have to go. Your time here is over, Jacob."

The boy took a step toward me, and I thought I saw a shadow dart behind him. A tall shadow. I heard Hannah yelp in pain beside me, but I kept my focus. She was still holding my hand, and I squeezed hers. She squeezed back to reassure me she was okay.

"Jacob, listen to me. I know that bad things happened in this house, that you saw bad things. I'm sorry that happened to you, but the bad things have to stop." The rocking horse flew across the room and broke into many pieces. I caught my breath and turned loose of Hannah's hand. I clutched Marisol's bear as if it were a life preserver. "I'm sorry about Mariana and Jameson, but it wasn't your fault. None of it was your fault. I don't know what happened to you, but I'm sorry."

The clock flew off the mantel and smashed on the floor, and a ball in the corner bounced furiously. The boy frowned and raised his face so that I could see him clearly. Yes, he was a terrifying sight, but at one time he had just been a boy. A boy who had been hurt by someone. A boy who had died here. The storm outside raged. Lightning smashed the darkness and illuminated the room in frantic flashes. But the thunder was strange, like it was happening in the house and not outside of it.

*Now what do I do? What should I say to this angry creature?* "Jacob, please believe me. Your brother's treasure is not yours to keep. You are not responsible for what he did; his crimes are not yours. I know you loved your brother, but what he did was wrong."

*Leave here.*

"I will not leave. This is my house now, along with everything in it. You have to go. I'm setting you free, Jacob. You don't have to stay and watch over Jameson's treasure anymore." He moved closer, but I stood my ground. "I promise you I'll take care of it. I won't let anything happen to it."

Hannah whispered beside me, "The energy is changing. He's used a lot of his strength. Command him to leave now, Jerica."

She was right; I could feel his power waning. Yes, I could command him to go, but my sympathy for him still grew. I got on my knees to get at eye level with him. "Jacob, you have to leave Summerleigh now. You can't stay here anymore. Go and take this treasure with you. It's my treasure, and I want you to have it." I held the stuffed animal out to him, my hands shaking, my heart pounding. Tears filled my eyes because I didn't really want to part with it...and I wasn't sure this was going to work. "It's okay. You can have it."

Everything got still. Jacob stepped closer to me. He was so close now that he could reach out and touch me if he wanted to. But he didn't. He touched the bear, and then he and the toy were gone. A quick flash of light filled the room, and then everything was as it had been. The room was empty and in need of repair.

Hannah was weeping, and I took her hand. The place was quiet. No more knocks and bangs. Even the wind outside stopped blowing. Somehow, we had achieved our goal. Summerleigh was finally free.

And so was I.

## *Chapter Nineteen—Harper*

After the funeral, Addison and I spent the rest of the day cleaning up the kitchen in the parlor. Miss Augustine stayed for a little while, but of course she didn't lift a finger. She did, however, fill her plate multiple times before unceremoniously leaving it on the kitchen table for me to wash.

I gave Momma another one of the pills the doctor prescribed for her and once again told her that was the last one. I had to, or else she would want the whole bottle. I still didn't trust that she wouldn't hurt herself. Several times in the past few days she'd called me Jeopardy, and once I caught her talking to herself (or someone) on the second-floor landing. Addison stayed close to me, and as I promised her, I slept in her room that night. She questioned me about a few things, including Aunt Dot's offer to come live with her, but agreed with me that the best thing to do now was to stay close to Momma.

"Everyone is gone now, Harper. Daddy, Jeopardy and now Grandfather. Promise me you'll never leave me."

"I promise you, Addison Lee. Wherever I go, you'll go too. Okay?"

I had a restless night that night but eventually fell asleep. After years of training, it was hard for me to sleep late; as usual, I got up before sunrise. I dressed quickly and went to the kitchen. I put on the percolator, mainly for myself because Addison didn't drink coffee and I had a feeling that Momma would not want any this morning. She'd probably drown her sorrows in cheap wine again. At least her supply was running out, and there was no one to take her to the store or buy her more. We hadn't seen hide nor hair of Dewey Landry, thankfully, and Momma sold her Chevy Master DeLuxe last week for some reason. God only knew what she'd done with the money. But if Aunt Dot proved right, we wouldn't need to depend on Momma anymore. What would that be like, to have food in the house and new clothes to wear whenever we wanted them?

"Harper?"

I nearly jumped out of my skin. Ben Hartley was calling me from the window. "What are you doing out here, Ben?"

"I thought you might want to go fishing. I've got the poles and stuff."

I was surprised to see him, what with everything that had passed between us earlier. I was kind of glad to see him...just not this early in the morning.

"Shouldn't you be getting ready for church?" I asked as I unlocked the back door and opened the screen to let him in.

"You going?"

"No. I don't go much anymore."

"Me either. I just thought we could fish. You know, like before. I'm sorry."

"You mean you're sorry you said what you said?" I asked him with my hands on my hips. "We hardly know each other, Ben Hartley. Do you go around telling all the girls you love them?"

"No. I've never done that. Just with you. But I won't say it again, I promise. I want to be your friend at least. Please go fishing with me."

I shrugged and said, "Okay, but only if Addison goes with us. I don't want to get a reputation."

"Okay," he agreed with a gap-toothed smile.

Addie wasn't up yet, which didn't bode well. That meant she wanted to sleep late. I tried to talk her into fishing, but she wasn't interested. "Go fishing, Harper. I'll be here."

I sighed and put my sneakers on. "All right, but I'll be back by ten. There's food in the refrigerator. Please eat something, Addie."

She agreed, and I left at the sound of her snoring.

Benny and I didn't talk much on the way to the river, but I could tell he was deep in thought. I wondered if I had made the right decision. I said I wouldn't go fishing with him again, but here I was. Was I so desperate to have friends that I would break my own rules? Well, Benny was a nice enough boy. We made it to the river just after sunrise, and he offered to bait my hook.

"No thanks. My daddy taught me how to fish."

"Did you like your dad?"

"Yes. Don't you like yours?"

He tossed his line in the water. "Nope. Not really."

Our luck was better today. I caught a speckled trout, and he snagged a redfish. His specimen outweighed mine, but at least he didn't brag about it. Not like Jeopardy would have. *Jeopardy. Here I am, having fun, and you're dead. You must be dead, or else I wouldn't have seen your ghost.* It was getting warm, so we retreated to a nearby shade tree to take a break from the heat. Benny offered me some of his soda pop, and I chugged a few swallows before handing the warm drink back to him. At least it was wet.

"What do you think y'all will do now? You aren't moving, are you?"

"What do you mean? Were you listening in on my conversation with Aunt Dot? That's not polite, you know." I didn't tell him I did it all the time.

"No. Of course not. I mean, now that your grandfather is dead, would you have to move? I mean, I guess he was taking care of y'all."

I wiped the sweat off my face. Benny asked the strangest and most inappropriate questions. "He didn't take care of us, Ben Hartley. You have some strange ideas."

My stomach was rumbling, and I was toying with the idea of going home. I was getting tired of Benny's company. Not because I didn't like him but because I'd gotten used to being alone. I liked it much more than I could have guessed. You got stronger when you were alone. I think that was a secret Jeopardy knew too.

Again Benny acted like he wanted to tell me something, but I didn't hurry him along. I hoped he wouldn't tell me he loved me again. I'd have to end our friendship if he talked crazy. "You won't have to worry about him anymore, Harper. He'll never hurt y'all again."

I launched to my feet. I had the creepy crawlies all over me, just like when that weird boy ghost popped up at Summerleigh. "What are you talking about?" He got up too and wiped his sweaty hands on his jeans. He wouldn't look at me. He looked at the river, at the grass, everywhere but at me. And that worried me. "What do you mean? You think you know something? Out with it, Ben Hartley."

"Why do you always do that? You think you're better than me? All I've tried to do is help you, Harper."

A rare wind caught the leaves overhead, and a few fluttered down between us. If it had been any other moment, it would have felt magical. This wasn't magical. Benny was trying to tell me something, something I didn't want to hear. But I had to listen. I had to listen good.

"How? How have you helped me? What do you know?" And just like that, as if someone had snapped their fingers, I knew too. I had figured it out a long time ago, and I just didn't want to admit it. My grandfather liked to hurt people in ways no one should.

Momma most of all.

Benny didn't answer me. He reached for the dingy wrapping on his hand, and my stomach did a double clutch like Daddy's old truck.

"How did you do that to your hand? Let me see it." I stepped toward him. I loomed over him now. I hadn't realized how much taller I was than him, but he didn't back down.

"Fine. You want to see it?" He unwrapped it furiously and held it up so I could see the angry red gashes. "I didn't mean to do it, Harper."

"You killed him, Benny. You killed Mr. Daughdrill. Why?"

He sobbed, and his eyes shone with tears. "I love you, Harper. I know I'm not supposed to say it, but I do. I just wanted to talk to him, to tell him to leave you and Addison alone. Everyone knows, Harper. Everyone knows what he is, but they didn't do anything." He was shouting now, and I was afraid of him. I'd never been afraid of him before. "Don't look at me like that. I didn't mean for it to happen."

"You stabbed him, Benny. Where did you get the scissors?" Those creepy crawlies were on me like white on rice.

"I was just going to talk to him. I went to his house to talk to him man to man, but he didn't come to the door. I tried the handle, and the door was open. I

remember opening the door and going in, but I
don't remember nothing after that. I think he yelled
at me, but it's like it was a dream. Next thing I knew,
I was holding the scissors, and then they were pok-
ing out of his chest. Honest, Harper. You have to believe me."

"You killed him, Benny. You killed him. You're a
murderer!"

"I did it for you, Harper. I swear I didn't plan on it.
It just happened."

I took off running. I cried and screamed, hoping
someone would hear me. I'd never been more scared
in all my life. I was friends with a murderer. Ben
Hartley killed Mr. Daughdrill. He might say he did it
for me, but that didn't make it right.

"Harper, wait! Please, wait! I love you, Harper
Belle!"

I'd never run so fast. By the time I made it home, my
legs were burning and I couldn't hardly breathe. I
raced past Momma and picked up the phone.

"Harper, what is it?" Addison asked as she came in
from the parlor.

I dropped the phone because I was shaking so bad.
Addison helped me to the chair while Momma got
me a glass of water.

And in that moment, I knew I couldn't do it. I
couldn't turn in my friend. He was no serial killer,
no psychotic murderer. He was a boy who wanted to
help me. He'd been influenced by this house, by the

spirits here, and had become an unwilling vessel for their evil. I hung the phone up. I never spoke about it again to anyone, not even Ben when I talked to him years later. Things were settled between us. He had helped me with something that I would never have had the courage to ask. But I believed that Ben didn't know what he was doing that night.

The damage had already been done, but we were free.

The sheriff came back to our house again that day. At first, I thought it was because he knew the truth about Benny, but that wasn't it. Dewey Landry had been arrested for shooting up Aunt Dot's house and trying to kill her. He'd been caught trying to leave town with a stash of money in a black bag. There were rumors that Momma had put him up to it.

Momma denied everything, but six months later she was ordered to undergo treatment at Searcy Mental Hospital and I never saw her again. Aunt Dot agreed to move back into Summerleigh with us. The state made her our legal guardian, and for the next ten years, we lived happily together there. Then each one of us slowly drifted apart as we all made our own lives. Aunt Dot died not long after Loxley married and moved away. Loxley had been the baby Aunt Dot had never had. She loved us all, but we knew she loved Loxley a little bit more. And we were okay with that.

There was plenty of love in this house now. Plenty of peace. Plenty of everything.

## *Chapter Twenty—Jerica*

*Mommy, wake up.* And I did. I shot right up in bed and immediately knew I was not alone in my bedroom. That's when I saw the dark figure sitting in the painted wooden chair near my door. He looked like a statue just sitting there watching me. Yes, it was true—Ben Hartley was sitting in my room. It wasn't quite morning yet, but I heard roosters crowing in the distance and the air had that strange kind of strawberry-colored glow that let you know the sun was about to appear.

How long had he been here? All night? I glanced at my nightstand and was relieved to see that there were no scissors lying there, but that didn't make me feel more comfortable.

"What are you doing in here, Ben? How did you get in?" That was kind of a stupid question since he lived here before I did. He must have still had a key.

He didn't answer me, not at first. "I tried to explain to you; I wanted you to know how important it was. You needed to leave, but you didn't listen to me. I told you to let sleeping dogs lie. It's not that I'm afraid of going to jail. I don't think I'll live another year, so what's to fear? It's just that I don't remember any of it. What I told Harper was the truth. One minute I was walking into Mr. Daughdrill's house, and then the next thing I know, I have blood on my hands. Not just his blood but mine too. I cut him so savagely that I cut myself in the process."

"Ben, you shouldn't be telling me this. Why are you here?"

Ben looked off into the distance, and I quickly grabbed my phone off the nightstand. He didn't seem to notice. I carefully pulled up Jesse's number and tapped on the screen.

"Everyone knew what he was doing to those girls. The whole town knew. And nobody did anything about it. I couldn't prove that he killed Jeopardy, but I saw him pulling up in that big black car of his and dropping Harper off at school. He wanted to do what he always did, but she fought back. I saw her do that and knew she was the one for me. She wasn't going to die, not like the other one. And I wasn't going to let it happen."

I could hear Jesse calling my name on the phone, and I surreptitiously turned down the volume. I said loudly so that Jesse could hear me, "Ben Hartley, you cannot be in my bedroom."

Ben got up out of his chair and walked over to me. He knelt down in front of me and took my hand. "I don't want to hurt you, Harper. I never wanted that. It's this place. Ever since I came here, I haven't been the same. When I used to live here, I would wake up sometimes and find myself walking the halls of Summerleigh. And I wouldn't even know how I got there. It's like it cursed me or something. It has control over me, and I don't want it anymore. I can't live with it anymore. I did the wrong thing, and I'm not even sure how I did it. I swear to you, Harper. I loved you then, and I love you now. Please forgive me for what I'm about to do."

I leaped off the opposite side of the bed and plastered myself against the wall. "No, Ben." I reminded myself to remain calm. "Don't do anything you're going to regret. Please, go home. Or go to the hospital, and I will meet you there. I'm a nurse, remember? You need help, and I can help you. Please, let me help you."

He smiled at me and shook his head. "There's no time for that now. I'm sorry, Harper. I will always love you." And then he left my room and I heard his footsteps going down the stairs. From my window, I watched Ben walk to Summerleigh, and he had something in his hand. What was it?

Oh God! It was a gas can! What was Ben planning to do?

I picked up the phone, surprised to hear Jesse still there. "Jesse! Ben has some gas, and I think he's going to burn down Summerleigh! I have to call the police!" I hung up the phone and immediately dialed 911.

"911. What is your emergency?"

"My house! Ben! He's trying to burn down my house!"

"What is your address?"

I gave the dispatcher the address but refused to answer any more questions. I could already see smoke pouring out of the bottom floor of the house. And Ben never came out.

I was in a pair of pajama shorts and a t-shirt, but it didn't matter. I had to get him out of there. He was out of his head—what if he killed himself trying to set the place on fire? I would never be able to live with myself if I let him die. I ran down the stairs and slid my feet into tennis shoes. I raced to the back door of Summerleigh, but Ben had locked it. I ran to the front door and found it was locked as well. I began to scream, "Ben! Open the door!" I could hear him crying and talking to himself or someone. I pounded and pounded, but he never came to the front door.

*Now what do I do?*

My eyes fell on a large rock. I picked it up and put it through one of the Great Room windows. Glass shattered everywhere, and I carefully reached inside and undid the latch. I slid the window up and climbed through without cutting myself too much.

"Ben? Please, come out now. Before it's too late."

I searched the entire bottom floor and found him nowhere. The kitchen was on fire, and one of the bedrooms—the one that had the mattresses stacked against the wall—was burning. Smoke was beginning to fill up the place, and all the windows had been closed.

I raced up the stairs searching for Ben. Suddenly, he was there in front of me and sloshed gasoline on the front of my shirt. "Jerica! You cannot be in here.

You aren't supposed to be here. I wanted to save you. You must leave now!" And then he took off, running as fast as any man half his age. He ran up the steps of the attic, went into the castle room and slammed the door. I could hear it lock as I raced up the steps and banged on the door. I listened carefully and heard the gasoline sloshing around. If I let him do this, if he succeeded in setting the attic on fire, he would certainly kill himself.

*Okay, Jerica. You are a nurse. You can handle this. Talk him down. Be calm and talk rationally.*

"Ben, you have to open this door. If you don't, you are going to hurt yourself, and you're going to make it really hard for people like me to help you. Please, stop what you're doing." No reply.

Okay, forget logical. Forget rational. I was going to have to lie to him just to save his life. "Ben Hartley, Harper's going to be so mad at you when she finds out you did this. She loves this place, and if you destroy it, she is never going to forgive you."

Ben came to the door and opened it slightly. As he did, smoke poured out of the room. I had to get him out of there fast.

"Ben, you don't want to miss a chance to see Harper. She's waiting for you downstairs. Just come with me, and I will take you to her. No. Leave that gas can here. She wants to talk to you."

"Really?" His excited face encouraged me. "Yes, take me to her."

Smoke was beginning to fill the hallway, and I had a strong urge to cough. I put one hand over my mouth and reached out my other hand for Ben's. He allowed me to take his hand, and we both coughed as we walked down the hall quickly. Or as quickly as he would move with me. "Are you sure she's not mad at me?" He coughed his question out.

"No, she's not mad at you. In fact, I know she loves you, Ben. She's waiting for you."

"She loves me? She said that? She loves me?" He was smiling from ear to ear.

We were coming down the stairs now. Just a few more steps and I would have him out of the house. I could see that he had left the key in the front door. And that way had less smoke than the back, so it seemed an obvious choice.

"Where is she, Jerica? You said she'd be here. Where is she?" He became agitated very quickly, another sign of the Alzheimer's that I suspected he had.

"On the front porch, Ben. She couldn't wait in here because it was too smoky. Come on, just a few more steps." I tugged at his hand, but he pulled away. I was losing him. He didn't believe me, and even in the smoke I could see that the madness was taking him again. The horrible madness, the disease that had taken so many.

He shook his head. "You said Harper was here. I know where she is. I know where she always is. She's in the kitchen. Right? Is she hiding in the kitchen?" And then he bolted and ran into the fiery furnace he'd created.

I screamed his name, but it did no good. There was so much heat coming from the kitchen that I would not survive entering it. I was still screaming when Jesse ran into the house. He too tried to reach Ben, but the old man didn't seem to hear us.

He kept yelling for Harper until his calls became screams, and then we heard nothing else. We knew that Ben Hartley was dead. He had killed himself in the most horrible way, completely out of his mind. Covered in smoke and wrapped in an emergency blanket, I sat in the back of the ambulance and watched as Summerleigh burned. The Volunteer Fire Department of George County did a good job of putting out the fire. They came pretty fast to the scene, but the damage was done.

Summerleigh would never be the same, and it had taken its last victim.

I vowed then and there to do just as Harper had done. I would keep Ben Hartley's secret for the rest of my life. I would tell no one, not even Jesse. That's the way Harper wanted it. I knew that.

I didn't stay at the caretaker's cottage. I took Jesse up on his offer and spent several weeks at his house thinking of nothing and doing nothing except working on his boat. It was nice to pretend that we were a family.

Jesse and me...and Marisol. She liked this place too.

# *Epilogue—Jerica*

"Are you sure you want to return to Summerleigh? It's a mess, Jerica. I didn't want to tell you this, but I went by there the other day, and it is truly a mess."

I sighed and kissed his cheek. "Yes, but it's my mess. I can't keep ignoring this. I have to see how bad it is. I've got some decisions to make, and I want you with me."

He kissed me back. "That's all you had to say. Let's load up. Put your work boots on, though. It's pretty bad in some places. Will you grab my camera? It's on the dresser in the guest room. Your room."

"Sure," I said with a smile. Yeah, I was ready to do this. I couldn't put it off forever. I'd gotten some emails from the insurance company, and from what I saw, they'd been pretty generous. So it would be possible to rebuild if that's what I wanted to do. But that was a big if. Jesse's camera was not on the dresser, so I opened the top drawer. Maybe he meant inside the dresser? Sure enough, it was there, and so was one other thing. I reached in and grabbed the camera and also the packet of letters tied with the pink ribbon. The letters addressed to Dorothy Daughdrill. I had brought them here from the caretaker's cottage but hadn't had the nerve to look at them yet. With shaking fingers, I untied the knot and removed one of the letters.

I slid the delicate paper out of the envelope. There was an address on the back, a military address, and I knew immediately that this letter was from John Jeffrey Belle.

*Dear Dorothy,*

*I hope this letter finds you well, for it has brought me much hope to receive yours. To know that you love me no matter what your father says, that you love me above all others...well, it is more than I deserve. Ever since I first met you, I knew you were the one. You are the love of my life, and I will love no other. Not as long as I have breath in my body. I pray this war ends soon so that I can come back to you and all my Belle girls. I know you worry about Ann, you worry about your father, but you shouldn't. We love each other, and that's all that matters. If your father hadn't interfered in the beginning, none of this would've happened. Just think, it's taken us ten years to discover the truth of what happened that night. I believed that you stood me up, that you left me there at the altar. What a fool I was. I'm sorry, Dorothy. I'm sorry I didn't wait for you, but I'm going to spend the rest of my life making it up to you.*

*All my love,*

*John Jeffrey Belle*

I stared at the letter and read it again and again. Jesse came in looking for me and found me reading the rest of them. I'd arranged them on the bed and read every single one. After the last one, I leaned back on the pillow, closed my eyes and sighed.

"This is horrible. What Mr. Daughdrill put those girls through, it's unreal. All this time, John Belle had been in love with Dot. And he believed them—Ann and her father, I mean—when they said that Dorothy had rejected him. And that she didn't want Jeopardy. Jeopardy was really Dorothy and John Jeffrey Belle's daughter. That's why Ann hated her so much. And that's why she was so willing to allow Mr. Daughdrill..."

Jesse shook his head in disgust. "Yeah, all of that. Talk about star-crossed lovers. They didn't have a chance."

I folded up all the letters, put them back in a stack and tied them up with the ribbon. "Let's put this away and forget about it. And I can tell you what I'm gonna do. I am going to rebuild Summerleigh. It is going to be the most beautiful, happiest bed-and-breakfast that George County has ever seen."

Jesse smiled and said, "I like that idea. I like it a lot."

"Can't do it by myself. You on board?"

"Do you really have to ask?"

Fifteen minutes later, we were back at Summerleigh. I was surprised to see that much of the house remained intact despite significant fire and smoke damage. We walked around the building carefully and made a mental punch list of where we needed to start on this new project.

"Forget this. I'm never gonna be able to remember all this. Let me go to the truck and grab a notebook."

"I thought writers could remember everything," I joked with him.

He didn't even turn around when he replied, "No, that's why we need notebooks. Be right back."

I heard a sound to my right coming from the bedroom hallway. I walked into the hallway and immediately saw my daughter. Marisol wore a yellow dress with a yellow ribbon in her hair. In life, I'd never seen her wear anything like that. Clearly, someone was helping her dress. And then Jeopardy stepped out of the room and stood behind her. I stared at them both and smiled.

"It's okay, baby. You can go play with Jeopardy. Mommy is okay." She took Jeopardy's hand, and they turned away from me and walked toward the back wall and then right through it. I went to Ann's old bedroom. It was the only room that didn't have any fire damage, and the window there was intact. From the window, I could see the two girls running together, hand in hand.

And then they disappeared. And I knew I would never see Marisol again. Not in this lifetime.

And I was okay.

# Read more from M.L. Bullock

*The Seven Sisters Series*

Seven Sisters
Moonlight Falls on Seven Sisters
Shadows Stir at Seven Sisters
The Stars that Fell
The Stars We Walked Upon
The Sun Rises Over Seven Sisters

*The Idlewood Series*

The Ghosts of Idlewood
Dreams of Idlewood
The Whispering Saint
The Haunted Child

*Return to Seven Sisters*
*(A Sequel Series to Seven Sisters)*

The Roses of Mobile
All the Summer Roses

*The Gulf Coast Paranormal Series*

The Ghosts of Kali Oka Road
The Ghosts of the Crescent Theater
A Haunting at Bloodgood Row
The Legend of the Ghost Queen
A Haunting at Dixie House
The Ghost Lights of Forrest Field
The Ghost of Gabrielle Bonet
The Ghost of Harrington Farm

*Shabby Hearts Paranormal Cozy Mystery Series*

A Touch of Shabby

To receive updates on her latest releases,
visit her website at MLBullock.com
and subscribe to her mailing list.

Made in the USA
San Bernardino, CA
24 August 2018